THE MUSTANGERS

A WESTERN STORY

THE MUSTANGERS

A WESTERN STORY

LAURAN PAINE

Thorndike Press • Chivers Press
Thorndike, Maine USA   Bath, England

This Large Print edition is published by Thorndike Press, USA and by Chivers Press, England.

Published in 2000 in the U.S. by arrangement with Golden West Literary Agency.

Published in 2000 in the U.K. by arrangement with Golden West Literary Agency.

U.S. Hardcover 0-7862-1586-0 (Western Series Edition)
U.K. Hardcover 0-7540-4279-0 (Chivers Large Print)
U.K. Softcover 0-7540-4280-4 (Camden Large Print)

The text of this Large Print edition is unabridged.
Other aspects of the book may vary from the original edition.

Set in 16 pt. Plantin by Al Chase.

Printed in the United States on permanent paper.

British Library Cataloguing-in-Publication Data available

Library of Congress Cataloging-in-Publication Data
Paine, Lauran.
   Mustangers : a Western story / Lauran Paine.
      p. cm.
   ISBN 0-7862-1586-0 (lg. print : hc : alk. paper)
   1. Horsemen and horsewomen — Fiction. 2. Wild horses
— Fiction. 3. Arizona — Fiction. 4. Mexico — Fiction.
5. Large type books. I. Title.
PS3566.A34 M89 2000
813′.54—dc21   00-034371

THE MUSTANGERS

CHAPTER ONE
THE MUSTANGERS

With the first cake ice on ponds and troughs it was time to head south. Leaving the high country with its forested giants, its creeks of clear, cold water, graze, and browse enough for ten times the number of cattle, even the shy little columbines in their shaded places. And the folks. They'd ridden for Amos Woods and his wife a full season. It was like the parting of family. Twelve-year-old Michelle-Marie, tough as old rawhide, with freckles and a wide mouth didn't make a sound as she wiped her eyes three times.

Rolling bedrolls, filling saddlebags, getting paid off, and a high wave always meant an end of something, not just summer, eating at the same table, laughing, teasing, working hard. Heading toward the wide, old stage road with soiled clouds above and one of those chill winds places like Wyoming and Colorado were cursed with at summer's end, they rode buttoned to the gullet, and, when they bore south beyond the village of Cache le Poudre, the wind was bitterly cold even through their buffalo coats.

Reg said: "The Woodses were good folks."

His partner agreed and added more. "An' Michelle-Marie was soft on you."

Reg's head swung inside his high-buttoned collar. "She's nine years old, for chris' sake!"

"She's twelve goin' onto thirteen."

They made it another eight or ten miles. Wintery nights in high country don't bother with dusk; they just get dark. It was a long ride, but as long as a person kept southerly, he'd eventually reach territory where it didn't freeze up every night as hard as a witch's teat.

Some years winter came early. This year it didn't. They had to forage as they went and made it as far south as Utah without getting caught by one of winter's early blasts with snow hip-pocket high on a tall Indian. Neither of them knew Utah. It just happened to be in the way as they continued undeviatingly southward. They knew New Mexico, Arizona, as much of Texas as they couldn't avoid. What they knew about Utah was hearsay. It was the place of Mormons, and folks elsewhere fairly agreed Mormons were different. These were the charitable folks.

They'd been on the trail a fair distance before they saw mountains higher than they'd ought to be and occasional ranches, mostly far apart with twin-rut roads meandering into respectable distances. It was customary to avoid towns except for supplies. In Utah avoiding towns was less of a problem than avoiding those far-out, isolated homesteads.

They met people, nodded, and got nods back. Nods but no smiles. Reg said: "Well, hell, at least there's no wind."

They were in livestock country but not on the Wyoming-Colorado scale. There were more farmed fields, more straight lines as though Utahans knew where property lines were. Millions of acres, thousands of miles — and no settler farmed a yard past an invisible line between himself and neighbors. This wasn't completely unusual, but where they'd worked the last few years, while there were occasional farms, mostly of homesteaders, they were rare, and farmed land didn't follow straight lines.

They camped on a slight lift where one scraggly tree stood. The feed was about stirrup high, and there was water. They made a twig fire, hobbled the horses, flattened bedrolls, and sat. It was silent enough to hear a shooting star. Reg looked at his partner. "Ten more days?"

Lane shrugged. Distance didn't matter as

long as it was southward, away from high-country winters. He said: "You notice how those folks we passed looked sort of bristly?"

"Yeah. You know anything about Mormons?"

"Well, the same things you've heard."

"Did you know they don't like fellers who wear black hats?"

Lane stared. "Black hats? What difference does the color . . . ?"

"Because those as aren't Mormons . . . mostly from places like California . . . wear black hats, an' Mormons don't like no one outside their territory."

"Where'd you hear that? Black hats . . . ?"

"Give me a fistful of that ripgut you're sittin' on. I'll clean the fry pan."

As Lane complied, he said: "I've had reasons for dislikin' some folks, but the color hat they wear had nothin' to do with it."

Reg worked, scouring their fry pan, and said nothing until he was satisfied and put the pan aside, face down. "If we don't bear southwesterly, we're goin' to be on the reservation. White-eyes aren't supposed to be there."

Lane kicked out of his boots preparatory to climbing into his blankets. "Bear more southwesterly," he said.

The following morning, although the sun arrived, there was a scattering of ragged, white clouds with soiled edges preceded by one of those ground-hugging, little gusty winds. It was hard to make breakfast, but that wasn't discouraging. Men ate, when they could, and went tucked up between times.

They skirted wide around a settlement called St. George, bearing steadily southward. There were distant houses, mostly old with curled siding, railless porches, and square enough to be wooden boxes. They avoided them, too. Lane said there was something in the air, something not exactly threatening but unfriendly.

Reg grinned. "Turn your hat inside out."

Lane did no such thing. As they passed one of those warped-sided, square houses, he wagged his head. The place seemed deserted. There wasn't even a dog. A thin spindrift of smoke rose from an overhead stovepipe, so someone was in there. There was also a man outside, curving around the northerly corner, watching the strangers pass. When it was safe, he darted to the porch, poked his head inside, and breathlessly said one word, closed the door, and vanished back the way he had come.

A lanky, rawboned man left the house by

11

the rear door, told a dark man to get his horse and saddle it, then returned to the house. Out back was a windmill and a wooden catchment with leaky seams. Grass grew around its base. That was where the dark man caught the horse and led it to a shed to be rigged out.

Those raggedy clouds were of interest for two reasons. If they had rain in them, and from their dirty appearance that seemed likely, they had to do a lot of closing up to make thunderheads, and if they did that. . . . Lane shook his head. "They're bearin' sort of northerly and around behind that town back yonder."

Reg wasn't convinced. He was still looking up, when he said: "Did you see that sign back yonder?"

"Sign?"

"That town was named Saint George. I'd as leave it didn't rain . . . my ground cloth leaks."

The country below St. George seemed to open, widen, and went southward farther than a man could see. It wasn't exactly ugly, but it lacked a lot of being like the high country up north. There were boulders the size of a horse, scrub brush, buffalo grass in clumps, and what looked to be a low-roofed barn far ahead. They followed twin ruts that

12

passed as a road. The ruts seemed to head for that distant structure.

Lane spat. "If that's a barn, where'd they get the wood?"

Reg was building a smoke, when he answered. "Can't be a barn. Maybe someone lives down there."

They saw a low rise westerly of the road. It was time to quit for the day. The rise had a withered, old, dead tree on it. They left the road. Lane pointed. "Cow tracks." Before they reached the rise, they also saw horse sign, a considerable amount of it.

Atop the low hill, as they were hobbling before off-saddling, Reg said: "It'd take a mile of this country for one cow . . . those horse tracks? . . . no shoes."

Lane watched his animal drop down, roll over and back, and arise to shake like a dog coming out of a creek. "Wild horses?"

Reg stood looking southward as he mused aloud. "You remember that song Percy Meek used to sing?" He waved his hand. "The devil in hell, we are told, was chained for a thousand years, an' there remained. The Lord set him free an' gave him Texas for his very own hell. Well, this isn't Texas, but it's close enough." As he faced around he said: "Barefoot horses?"

Lane shrugged. "Reservation's down

there somewhere."

They went about gathering twigs for a supper fire. Those ragged clouds didn't come together. They thinned out over the mountainous country up by St. George. They discussed that house back yonder where the scrub-brush land went up to the porch. They also speculated about that ramshackle, distant barn, or whatever it was. They would find out eventually by following the ruts. It was a store, and its location was known as Wolf Hole, run by a woman with a disposition of a bear with a sore behind and her coarse-featured, freckled daughter.

Dawn light made visibility perfect. It showed hundreds of miles of nothing in three directions. Northward, back up in the St. George country, there were those great mountains. It hadn't frozen the last few nights, so they struck camp late. The sun was climbing when they left the dead-tree hillock, and, when they'd been in the saddle a couple of hours, Lane raised a stiff arm.

Westerly was a scattering of cottonwoods. For some distance around there was stirrup-high ripgut, buffalo grass, and thistle. They could make out that building down yonder, but the greenery was more promising, so they headed for it.

It was one of those rare sightings in stony, summer-scorched, ugly country — a sump spring that fed the greenery. Every kind of critter watered at this place. Cattle and horses did a professional job of grazing. Only the thistles flourished without being eaten. There was what once had been a fagot corral, no gate, just a large circling where wrist-size, long-dead lengths of native wood lay in the grass. There wasn't a straight fagot or a short one. Barefoot horses and cattle had been stepping over that wood since time out of mind. That kind of scantling wood didn't rot; it just got harder.

Lane thought they should camp there, although it was still early. To make his point he jutted his jaw. There was not another cottonwood tree as far as a man could see, and most likely no water.

Reg was agreeable, as much for the graze as for the diminished possibility of rain. There were croaker frogs, and, while the partners had usually foraged, those bloated, ugly frogs were perfectly safe. They'd heard once up near Laramie that the French ate frogs. A schoolteacher had told them that. At this oasis with the sound of horses eating Reg said: "Anyone who'd eat something like that's got to be downright depraved."

15

Lane looked at his partner. "Depraved?"

Reg was studying tracks and wouldn't be ruffled. "Look there. Real small hoofs. Too small for ridin'."

Lane didn't look. He nursed a spindly fire to life. They ate with the sun reddening off in the west and frogs making unpleasant sounds. They decided in the morning they would ride yonder to that old barn. Where there are barns, there are people, but a casual look in all directions showed no sign of houses, just the land that rolled and dipped. It looked flat, but it wasn't. There could be more of those box houses.

Sometime in the night they were awakened by a plodding line of bony cattle heading for the sump spring, indifferent to the scent of humans in the dark. The men sat up and watched. The light was poor, but it wasn't necessary to have good sight to see cattle pass, thin and thirsty.

Reg said: "Old gummers."

Lane agreed. There was abundant feed in all directions. Even if they'd shed most of their grinders, they had ought to be in better flesh.

Reg was lowering himself to the blankets when he said — "Wormy." — and heaved up onto one side.

He was right, but by dawn light the cattle

had tanked up and departed, so it didn't matter whether he was right or not. While they were cleaning up at the spring, Reg mentioned staying in this place for a day or two, and, while his partner neither agreed nor disagreed, he had unkind words for cattle on green feed filling up on water that made walking barefoot a hazardous enterprise.

Lane was curious about that old, ramshackle barn. They were speculating when the glass-clear air carried a sound familiar to horsemen, a shod horse striking a stone. They faced around to watch three riders, heading in their direction. Two were large men. They rode together. The third rider hung back a yard or so. The large men were riding big, pudding-hoofed, farm horses.

Lane said: "We're trespassin'."

Reg snorted derisively without speaking. There was no question the riders were coming directly toward them, and they neither threw the high wave of friendship nor smiled. Where they dismounted and handed the dark, third man their reins, the third horseman's mount pawed, threw its head, and switched its tail. Horsemen didn't ride mares for exactly this reason. The dark man's animal was a mare, a horsing mare. Horsing mares were reliable

17

except for the three days every month when they "came in." Then they bit, rubbed their rears on fence posts, kicked, and picked fights with other horses.

One of the men had pale eyes and grin wrinkles. When they were close, he said: "This here is Todd Kingman. I'm Josiah Stearn."

Lane introduced himself and Reg Bachelor. There were no handshakes. Nothing was said of the dark man back yonder with his horsing mare who looked like a kind of tame Indian.

Josiah Stearn was guardedly friendly. He asked where the partners were heading.

Reg answered shortly. "New Mexico. We been in the high country. Too cold."

Josiah Stearn picked up a twig and was examining it, when the other large man asked a question. "Did you ever run wild horses?"

Before Reg could truthfully answer, his partner said: "We've run 'em."

The big men exchanged a glance. During the interval Lane's assessment of Todd Kingman was firming up. It wasn't complimentary.

Josiah Stearn snapped the twig and dropped it. "We was wonderin' if you boys'd help us with a problem. We got too many wild horses competin' with our cattle for feed."

Lane was building a smoke, when he said: "We haven't seen any wild horses. We saw some bony cattle." It wasn't a tactful thing to say, but Lane smiled at the man named Kingman and waited.

Kingman wouldn't be baited.

Josiah Stearn got things back where he wanted them. "These wild horses . . . all you see is their dust. Mister Kingman's got an offer for you. We'll supply the saddle stock for you . . . three to each of you . . . an' we'll buy every mustang you catch an' pay top price. Ninety cents a head."

Where it was possible to deliver wild horses to a reduction works, they brought two dollars a head. In the Wolf Hole country with no way to transport wild horses — Lane looked at his partner.

Reg Bachelor's lifelong habit of being unable to conceal dislike showed clearly, when he ignored the pale-eyed man and spoke directly to Todd Kingman. "Dollar a head. You furnish horses 'n' feed for 'em."

Kingman's expression hadn't changed. It was set in stone.

Josiah Stearn said: "We'll loan you a man. He knows the country. Mister Bachelor, them horses is wilder'n a March hare. Indians call 'em ghost horses."

Reg almost smiled. "Mister Kingman . . . ?"

"A dollar a head," Kingman said, and turned to walk back to his horse.

Josiah Stearn fidgeted. Bachelor put his gaze on Stearn, when he said: "This feller you'll loan us . . . is he a Mormon?"

Stearn's face showed a faint rise in color, but his answer was softly given. "His name's James Lee. He's a Mormon . . . Mister Bachelor, you got somethin' against Mormons?"

"No. Never knew any until now."

Stearn returned to his horse. The three men mounted and without a rearward glance rode back the way they had come, with the dark man in the rear having trouble with his horsing mare.

CHAPTER TWO
SETTLING IN — AND DOWN

Reg went into some shade, sat down, and looked up. "We were headin' for New Mexico."

Lane colored. "We only got nine dollars between us, an' they'll furnish the horses." Lane sank down in the same shade. "We only got to catch a dozen head to get travelin' money."

"You never ran wild horses in your misbegotten life."

Lane nodded. "We might get lucky an' catch thirty, forty. At a dollar a head that'd be. . . ."

"Thirty dollars. Lane, you're crazy."

"Did you see what they were riding? Twelve-hundred-pound plow horses. No wonder they got to hire someone to catch their mustangs."

Reg's mood only changed slightly, when he said: "Let's ride over to that barn." As he was rising to dust off, he added: "I don't like that Kingman feller." He turned abruptly. "We didn't shake hands."

Lane was up and bridling his animal.

"When they come back." He snugged up the cinch, swung aboard, and, as he was evening up his reins, he said: "Maybe this Lee feller's run wild horses."

To the weathered, large building wasn't much of a ride. As they got closer, it was obvious the building wasn't a barn. There were no corrals, no snubbing poles, only a hitch rack of sorts. As they tied up, a red-headed girl came to the doorway. They smiled. She smiled back.

Inside the store was gloomy. What impressed the partners was the inventory. Shelves were lined with tin goods. Overhead on bent spikes hung leather goods, a flank cinch stamped **N. Porter Saddle and Harness Company, Phoenix**. There were a stack of Navajo saddle blankets, some bits on nails in the wall, and a fair-size counter with a graying woman built like a sawdust barrel behind it. She said something curt, and the red-headed girl disappeared. To them the woman said: "Supplies?"

They spent three of their dollars, had no luck engaging the woman in conversation, went back outside, got astride, and headed back the way they had come. Reg said: "Who in hell would trade there?"

The answer was obvious. "Anyone who don't want to go ninety miles up to Saint

22

George," Lane replied, and sighed. "If I had the money, I'd buy me a brown hat."

Back at the camp Reg went to wash his horse's back. Lane stood looking in the direction of the Wolf Hole store. Eventually he went to sluice his horse off, hobbled it, and went to sit in the shade where Reg was building a smoke. Before licking the wheat straw paper, Reg said: "All the places I been I never ran into so much downright dislike."

Lane did not comment. There were two riders in the middle distance, each rider leading three horses. Reg fired up, blew smoke, followed his partner's gaze, and spat. "The Saints."

Todd Kingman was absent, but Josiah Stearn was recognizable. He was riding with a large, younger man. When Stearn was closer, he threw a high wave. Lane returned the greeting. Reg was concentrating on the led horses, eyes pinched nearly closed against smoke rising straight up.

They rose. The rider with Josiah Stearn was smiling. He had coarse features, small, blue eyes, and patches of almost sorrel hair sticking from beneath his hat brim. He was big. He was also muscled up. He dismounted, trailed lead shanks as he knelt to hobble his animal.

Stearn said: "Gents, this is James Lee. He

23

knows the country. Jim, that there is Mister Bachelor. The other feller . . . I don't remember."

Lane shrugged, shook hands with James Lee, and turned to examine the horses. There wasn't a mare among them, for which he was thankful. They looked reasonably sound. One was a pale gray. When Lane raised a hand, the gray pinned back its ears. Lane turned to Josiah Stearn. "Good broke horses are they, Mister Stearn?"

"We ride 'em," Stearn replied.

Reg who had also studied the horses spoke to the pale-eyed, older man. "That gray yours?"

"No. He belongs to Todd Kingman. He sent him along."

Reg considered the pair of big Mormons for a moment, then went to his bedroll, rummaged, shoved something into the front of his britches, arose, and walked back. The saw-handle butt of the six-gun was unavoidably visible. Jim Lee's smile wilted. Josiah Stearn ran his reins through both hands.

Reg said: "Mister Stearn, we need decent, sound animals."

"Like I said, Todd rides that horse. He's broke."

Reg barely let the older man finish before he spoke. "If you folks get us hurt, I'll blow your gawd-damned head . . . !"

"No cause for that kind of talk, Mister Bachelor." Josiah Stearn cleared his throat and half turned. "Jim, trade horses with 'em. I'll lead the gray back."

Lee grinned. "No need . . . I'll ride the gray." He turned his smile on the partners. "I know that gray. I've rode him."

Lane said: "What does he do?"

"Put a cold saddle blanket on him, an' he'll wait until you're up there, then he'll jump as high as he can. If you know he's goin' to do that, he don't buck. Just gives that almighty big jump."

"Anything else, Mister Lee?"

"Mister Lee's my pa. I'm Jim. One other thing . . . when you stick your foot in the stirrup, he'll turn real quick and nip your butt. All's a man's got to do, if he knows that, is keep a tight rein on the right side."

Reg approached the muscled-up, older man with the pale blue eyes and shoved out his hand. "Dollar a head . . . we'll keep the horses . . . you fetch feed for 'em. All right?"

Josiah Stearn said: "You sell what you catch to us."

They shook hands. Jim Lee went to remove his bedroll and saddlebags, took them into the shade, and dropped them. He watched Josiah Stearn ride back the way they had come, and smiled at his new companions. Jim Lee just naturally smiled. He was docile, helpful, one of those people it was hard not to like.

Over a spindly fire a few days later Jim told a story that the partners listened to like stone images. Jim's grandfather had been John Doyle Lee. He was caught over at Lee's Ferry, hiding in a chicken shed, when the soldiers came. John Doyle Lee was shot to death by an Army firing squad on a brisk, chilly day at Mountain Meadows, twenty years to the day after leading Indians and Mormons in an attack on a passing-through wagon train of Gentiles. Anyone not a Mormon was a Gentile. John Doyle Lee's last words were for the benefit of his wives and children. "Not in the face, boys." When they put him in the narrow, long box to be delivered to his family, his face hadn't been mutilated.

Jim not only knew the territory and Mrs. Dugan at the Wolf Hole store, he also had run wild horses. He said the Mormons had been trying for years to thin down the herd of mustangs. He said they shot some, and the reason they had no luck catching them was because mostly their saddle animals were big and powerful, just right for working the ground but worthless trying to catch wild horses.

Jim settled in. Both Reg and Lane liked him. One morning he pointed at some crooked, hard-as-iron fagots in the grass. "Mister Kingman, his Indian, and some others made a trap out of them pieces of wood to catch the mustangs. They caught two old gummer mares . . . never caught any more."

Lane had a question. "Do they belong to anyone? Isn't there a reservation down yonder somewhere?"

"Miles from here," Lee explained. "Mostly, they stay down there. Wild horses don't belong to no one. Catch 'em an' they're yours."

Jim Lee ate like a horse. Reg had forgot to ask Josiah Stearn about supplies. Lee smiled. "Over at the store she's got everything."

Lane was wiping both hands in the grass, when he said wryly: "Not friendly, is she?"

Jim's smile broadened. "Her husband died some time back. Gila monster bit him. Folks say she turned bitter. You met her?"

Lane nodded and shifted the subject. "Is this the only water?"

Lee nodded and also wiped supper grease in the grass. "For a long ways. They don't go to the river at Lee's Ferry . . . too many people." He brightened. "I'll tell you somethin' you already know, bein' mustangers. Mister Kingman wouldn't listen to me. Wild horses can scent up folks a mile. Mister Kingman set up camp behind this knoll."

Reg and Lane exchanged a look as Jim Lee arose to go yonder to wash and consider the hobbled horses. As Lane came up, Lee said: "Mind you keep the right rein tight or he'll nip your butt." He grinned. "He's tough, though."

Reg came up. "Those sticks came from Mister Kingman's trap?"

"Yeah. They're called iron wood." Lee's good-natured expression lingered. "You figure to make a trap here?" When Reg nodded and went to scuff among the iron wood fagots, he nearly fell when a boot got caught in wire. As he bent to free his foot, Jim called to him. "That wire's been lyin' out here for years. It might not be any good now."

Reg felt in the grass before slowly straightening up, looking at his partner. "It was wired in an' out from the ground to near the top."

"Only way to make it," Jim Lee said, "so's it'd give when scairt horses run into it.

There was nothin' wrong with the trap."

Reg returned to the camp, sank to the ground, considering the big-smiling Mormon. He felt for his tobacco poke and offered it. Lee shook his head. "Thanks all the same. We don't use tobacco or drink coffee. I got to pee."

The partners watched Lee walk away with his back to them. Reg said: "Don't smoke, drink coffee, and gawd knows what else."

The answer he got shocked him. "Lee told me Mister Kingman's got seven kids and three wives. One legal wife an' two cousins because it's against the law to have more'n one wife."

Reg went to work using swatches of bent grass to clean the fry pan. When Lee returned, he asked a point-blank question. "Mister Kingman's got three wives?"

Jim smiled and nodded. "Not supposed to any more. Years back before I was borned a man could have as many wives as he could look out for. The United States government made it against the law." Jim plucked a stalk and chewed it. "It didn't work. Some men had four, five wives. They couldn't just turn 'em out because someone back East said so."

Lane smiled. "So they called the extra wives cousins?"

Lee nodded. "Cousins, step-daughters . . . if they was old, called 'em mothers. The church went along with the back East government. One wife." His broad smile returned. "Them as wouldn't shed their extra wives . . . the church didn't say much . . . it couldn't . . . the elders had more'n one wife. But they called men who kept their plural wives Jack Mormons. Folks still call 'em that."

Reg recovered from his shock, finished with the fry pan, and said: "Mister Kingman's a Jack Mormon?"

Jim nodded. "In folks' eyes it isn't no sin. Brigham had a house full of 'em."

"Brigham Young?"

"He run the church years back. Made the Army back down."

Lane rolled a smoke. He and Reg gazed pensively at one another. Nothing more was said on this subject.

The following six days they moved camp eastward. Jim said wind came from the north. He had tried to explain that to his bishop, Mister Kingman. Mustangs traveled as much by scent as by sighting. Getting the old corral upright required digging post holes at intervals.

At night they ate early and bedded down.

The new camp was a long walk. It was also inconvenient. They had to carry water and firewood which wasn't plentiful. They were down to beans and spuds, when Josiah Stearn appeared, driving a battered and faded light dray wagon mounded with cured hay. Beneath the hay were provisions. He walked down to inspect the resurrected trap, walked back, spoke aside with Jim Lee, and hunkered across a little supper fire from the partners. He said: "You're makin' progress. Years back me 'n' some other gents set up that trap."

Reg nodded. "An' caught two old mares."

Stearn ruefully smiled. "Wild horses is hard to trap. Mexicans say they're *coyote,* an' they are for a fact." He accepted a tin plate of fried hoe cakes. "You goin' to make wings?"

Jim Lee nodded. "Use the same sticks an' wire, only wider this time."

Stearn looked where the horses were grazing. "Get along with the gray, do you?"

Reg answered. "Haven't ridden him yet."

After Stearn left, Reg shook his head. "Jim, it'd break his face to smile, wouldn't it?"

Lee broadly grinned without answering.

They finished the trap and widened its wings as much as Jim said they should be, then he said he'd go look for the horses. Reg would have gone with him, but Jim said better one mounted man than two, so they worked on the trap the following day. Jim didn't return for two days, and he brought a companion, a tall, thin Indian named Stachio who was as expressionless as Jim Lee was the opposite.

The Indian was hungry. As time passed, the partners learned something. Stachio was always hungry. He was wiry, rarely spoke, used a mixture of Navajo, Mexican Spanish, and English. He cut his words off. He and Jim Lee were old friends. There was a dark side to the Navajo, but he could read the sign of a fly over glass.

Jim and the Navajo were gone one morning when the partners came out of their blankets. One of them had taken the cranky gray horse. Reg shrugged. If they never returned, the partners wouldn't have lost anything. But they returned a little shy of sundown on the third day. They had located a band of mustangs.

They had done something else. They saw the dust first and made a wide sashay to get out and around it. When they were westerly, the mustangs picked up either their scent or movement and raced in the opposite direction. To a wild horse anything foreign was a threat. Unlike antelope they were not attracted by curiosity.

Jim and the Navajo sashayed a half day's ride northward then headed for the camp. Jim said the mustangs would be about six, eight miles from the trap. The Indian ate everything in sight, rarely looked at Reg and Lane, but showed that he understood what Jim said with an occasional slight jerk of his head up and down.

Lane wondered aloud if the four of them could split wide and come in behind the wild horses, ease them closer to the trap.

Jim smiled and shook his head. "They'd get the scent an' run back the way they come. They're wilder'n birds."

Stachio put in abruptly: "They know this place. We go long 'way off, set, an' wait."

Whatever else Stachio was deficient in, he knew wild horses. They lived off Josiah Stearn's bounty for two days, then went horse hunting again, and this time, although they spread wide and made an in-depth search, they did not even see dust. On the ride back the Mormon and the Navajo remained behind, talking in barely audible voices.

Lane and his partner were riding together on loose reins, when Reg said: "You get a feeling about this business?"

Lane shook his head. The day was ending. Their campsite was distantly visible. He was hungry. "The Indian saw mustangs. Jim sided with him. You 'n' me . . . well . . . seein' tracks isn't good enough."

"You mean the Navajo and Jim are playin' some kind of game with us?"

"Somethin' like that."

Lane looked at his partner. "You're always imaginin' things."

That remark brought a profanity spree. Both men were practiced and eloquent swearers. Not long after becoming partners they had formed a habit of cursing each other at the slightest excuse. Swearing among their kind was not only an art form, it eventually developed into an experienced, almost eloquent stretch of the English language and the imagination.

Jim Lee and the Indian listened, sure that the two partners would dismount and fight. It didn't happen. It had once happened. Both were physically strong. The problem was that neither could whip the other.

When they reached camp, had cared for the animals, Jim and the Navajo scattered to find wood, and Jim told the Indian one of them had ought to go tell Todd Kingman the partners were mad at each other and that most likely they wouldn't do what was necessary to catch horses. Stachio disappeared after supper.

Jim disingenuously smiled. "They do that now 'n' then. Go off by theirselves. He'll come back."

And he did come back, the following morning, cared for his animal, hunkered at the breakfast fire, did not look directly at the others, and was mute.

Reg told Lane he'd never trusted Indians. He'd bet new money Stachio had met some other tomahawks and just damned well might sneak in at night and steal everything that wasn't tied down.

Lane shook his head. "You're doin' it again, Reg."

"Doin' what?"

"Figurin' the worst."

That statement brought forth another profane outburst but this time not as long, and, when it subsided, Reg said: "All right, but I'll watch that Indian day 'n' night. . . ."

They went to saddle up for another day-long sashay. Jim Lee and the Indian went along. This time they saw dust less than three, four miles from the trap. They also saw a band of mostly white-faced cattle. The cattle gazed stoically and went back-picking. They agreed about something. Those Mormon cattle needed spraying and worming.

Stachio raised a rigid arm. The mustangs were grazing along, heads down, butts to the oncoming distant horsemen. It was the closest — the first time — the partners had got a good look.

It lasted only a few minutes. A stud horse threw up its head and trumpeted. Within moments the dust was too thick to see more than the rumps of the slower, older horses. Jim Lee and the Navajo grinned like tame apes. Jim said: "They're gettin' closer to the trap. If they don't scatter too far . . . the sump hole is the onliest water for a considerable distance."

Stachio made what for him was an oratorical spectacular. "Too bad we spooked 'em. They'd have smelt up the water an' got closer."

If the horses came back, it wouldn't be soon. The following day Reg saddled up early amid a slight chill below a high, soiled overcast. His partner, the Navajo, and Jim Lee were cleaning up.

Reg swung astride and gigged the Kingman horse. What ensued held the men on the ground as silent and still as stones. The horse sat back, hoisted himself into the air in a prodigious leap. When he came down, he was maybe ten, twelve feet from where he'd been. Reg was still up there, but, when that big horse came down stiff-legged, Reg's horsehair hatband was hurled to the ground a fair distance.

Reg gigged the horse. It moved out as though nothing had happened. It reined both ways, even backed in a straight line, and went in obedience to the reins back to the camp. Reg dismounted. A shirt button had popped loose. As he was fixing this, Stachio came up to hand over the hatband.

Reg buttoned, removed his hat to replace the horsehair band, put his hat on. "I'm goin' to kill that son-of-a-bitch."

Lane knew better, but he spoke anyway. "They told you he'd do that. Warm the blanket at the fire, Reg."

Bachelor was in no mood to overlook sound advice given condescendingly. He faced Lane. "I'll kill that son-of-a-bitchin' Mormon, too, an' you keep your gawd-damned preachin' to yourself."

Reg started toward his bedroll. He hadn't covered more than a yard, when his legs folded. He hung there on all fours, cussing a blue streak until Lane went over to hoist him back upright. Reg turned on his partner. "Mustangers! Every time you get a gawd-damned idea . . . help me set down."

Jim and the Navajo made it a point to find things to do nowhere near Bachelor. So did

Lane until Reg struggled to get upright, pointed, and swore a blue streak.

The flank cinch — called a poop strap — was hanging loose on both sides. "He broke my cinch, the son-of-a-bitch!"

Lane was placating. "That old woman at the store had one hangin' from the rafters. I'll ride over an' get it."

Reg looked disgustedly at his partner. "She'll want money."

"I got enough. Set, an' I'll be back directly. You all right?"

"I think my back's broke. That son-of-a-bitch came down stiff-legged. It was like sittin' atop a jackhammer."

Lane eased Reg down on his bedroll. "If your back was broke, you couldn't have walked."

"Is that so? You're a gawd-damned doctor?" Reg rose with an effort and started walking. He approached the Kingman horse, removed both halves of his flank cinch, faced the horse, and Lane held his breath. The Kingman horse wasn't hobbled. If Reg hit him, they'd never even see him again.

Jim Lee spoke to Bachelor. "I never seen that horse do that before."

Reg turned, still fisting the torn poop strap. "Mister Lee, that bastard Kingman

. . . I told him . . . you get one of us hurt on your gawd-damned Mormon horses, an' I'll kill you."

Jim Lee smiled broadly without speaking, and Lane got his first inkling about the big Mormon. He was good-natured, was helpful, was even likable, but that constant smiling . . . ? Lane went to saddle up for the ride to the Wolf Hole store.

Reg said — "I'm goin' with you." — and growled for Jim Lee to snug up the Kingman horse, which Lee did and handed the reins to Bachelor, widely smiling.

CHAPTER THREE
TRAPPED!

Reg shortened the right rein, toed in, rose up, and settled over leather, gritting his teeth.

Lane said: "If your back's hurt bad. . . ."

"Just ride!"

They covered the distance slowly. Jim Lee and the Indian watched in deep silence. The Navajo wasn't talkative, and while Jim was, this time he just watched and smiled as they rode out.

At the store they looped reins. Their approach had been from the west, behind the building where that red-headed girl was out back making kindling. She straightened up, and, when they'd waved, she raised a faltering hand to return the greeting and went inside out of sight.

The barrel-built woman named Dugan was swinging a feather duster like she was killing snakes. She turned, went behind the counter, and waited, unsmiling and silent.

Reg went to stand below the flank cinch suspended from above. He walked like a man with a hot potato in his britches. If the woman noticed, it didn't show in her expressionless face.

Lane leaned on the counter as he told her what had happened and that they needed a new flank cinch. Without a word she got a long pole with a hook, went over near Reg and, using the pole, hooked the cinch, lowered it, and returned with it to the counter. Reg went over to look at it.

The woman looked at Reg and said: "Five dollars."

Neither partner moved nor spoke. In the *Porter Catalog* the identical cinch was two dollars. The girl appeared silently in a shadowy doorway. Lane smiled. She smiled back, and, when an angry Reg Bachelor addressed the woman, the girl disappeared.

"Lady, in the catalog that cinch sells for two dollars."

She looked directly at Reg, expressionless except for the steely gaze. "Five dollars!"

Reg's color was increasing when Lane dug in a pocket, put five badly wrinkled, dog-eared, one-dollar bills on the counter, and picked up the poop strap. There was a better than even chance Reg would not need a poop strap. They were engaged in a business where their chances of roping an animal were about as possible as the sky falling.

Reg growled at the woman: "Don't touch

that money! Two gawd-damned dollars or you can hang it back up."

Mrs. Dugan reached for her pole, draped the cinch from its metal tip, marched over where the vacant bent nail was, and raised the pole. She rehung the cinch and marched back, putting the pole aside. "You got any idea how much it costs to get things hauled down here? This ain't Denver or wherever you're from. To get my mail and what-not I got to go up to Saint George. You know how far that is, Yankee?"

Reg said: "Yankee?"

"Yankee Gentile!"

Lane butted in. "He hurt his back. He needs that cinch to keep the cantle from comin' up an' hittin' where he hurts. Ma'am, three dollars?"

"You deef, Yankee? Five dollars!"

Reg sputtered. He'd rarely ever wanted to hit someone as much as he wanted to now. "Three dollars!"

Lane tried again. "Five dollars is about all we have."

She faced Lane. "If you're out of money, go back where you came from. What're you doin' down here, anyway?"

"Fixin' to catch wild horses for Josiah Stearn an' Todd Kingman."

"*Bishop* Kingman, Yankee!" The woman

straightened up off her counter, picked up her feather duster, and turned her back on the partners.

Lane saw a wisp of movement. The red-headed girl was partially hidden by a doorway. She had been eavesdropping. Lane made a final effort. "Four dollars?"

The woman was vigorously swinging her duster and neither spoke nor turned.

Outside the heat was increasing. Lane made a point of not watching Reg mount the gray horse, even up the reins with bulging jaw muscles, and head back the way they had come.

Halfway back Lane said: "You can use my poop strap."

"An' what'll you use!"

"As far as I can see right now, neither of us is goin' to do much ropin'."

Reg rode erectly. The Kingman horse went along on a loose rein. Whether he knew it or not, he was hiking in the correct direction. Reg said: "I wish she'd been a man. Lane, of all the places we've been this here is the ugliest an' most unfriendly."

When they reached camp, both the big Mormon and the Indian had news. Josiah Stearn and Todd Kingman were coming. Neither partner asked how Lee and Stachio knew this. They were occupied with caring

43

for their animals. Reg could not altogether suppress a groan, when he lifted away the saddle. Lane made a point of not hearing.

Jim broadly smiled as he asked Reg how the gray horse had behaved and got back a reluctantly given truthful reply. "Like a good horse. He's smart for a fact. Easy riding. Lane, you hungry?"

A half hour later, having eaten and enjoying a smoke, the Indian growled and pointed. A pair of riders was approaching from the north. Reg spat in his palm, killed the smoke, and leaned to rise. The best actor on earth couldn't have hidden the pain, and Reg Bachelor was not an actor by the longest stretch of the imagination.

With his back to the others, Reg went over to his bedroll, rummaged for the old six-gun, got off his knees, and shoved the gun under his belt and britches in back and returned to be with the others. The pair of horsemen came up, nodded, and dismounted.

Jim said — "I'll mind their horses." — and would have gone to do this, but Reg stopped him. "Let 'em mind their own horses . . . I know, he's a bishop. But down here he isn't. Stay here, Jim."

The two visitors led their animals, and each man trailed his reins as they sat on the ground. Kingman ignored the partners to address Jim Lee. "The trap looks good."

Jim was almost apologetic. "Everything we needed was on the ground. All's we had to do was set it up."

Kingman asked if any wild horses had been sighted, and Jim beamed because he could answer affirmatively.

Reg's back was killing him. He said: "Why'd you come down here?"

It wasn't just the abrupt way it had been said. It was also the strained, antagonistic way it had been said — almost as a challenge.

Before either visitor could speak, Reg said: "Mister Kingman, that gawd-damned gray horse like to broke my back. He busted my flank cinch into two pieces. That dumpy old hag at the store yonder's got a Porter flank cinch. Porter sells it for a couple of dollars. She said five dollars an' called us Yankees. We're not Yankees. Neither of us ever been east of the Missouri. Mister Kingman, that horse of yours busted my flank cinch."

Josiah Stearn spoke quickly. "We'll get you a cinch."

"What's the matter with that damned woman, Mister Stearn?"

"Her husband passed on a while back. They was close."

45

Lane spoke. "It's not just her, gents. The both of us never been in a place where bein' friendly don't come naturally."

The large, expressionless man almost smiled as he said: "Our folks was hounded and hurt by them as don't like our religion. We came out here to live free. It's hard."

Reg looked at Jim Lee. For once he wasn't smiling, and he didn't take his eyes off Todd Kingman.

Lane got the impression that, if Kingman had told Jim Lee to cut a throat, Jim would do it. He sighed, ignored the stone-faced man, and addressed Josiah Stearn. "All we figured to do was catch some wild horses. Neither one of us been inside a church since we were baptized. It doesn't help when we're surrounded by folks that hate us for what someone else did years back."

Josiah Stearn spread both work-hardened hands, palms up. "Out where you are, no-body's goin' to make trouble. Mostly folks don't even know you're here. How're the supplies holdin' up?"

Lane shrugged. "For a while yet, but we'll be out of feed for the horses directly."

Todd Kingman ended that conversation. "You fellers know what a proselyte is?"

They didn't, and Kingman didn't explain. "You'd be welcome into the church."

Reg rolled his eyes. Before he could say something inappropriate, Lane spoke. "Right now it's wild horses, Mister Kingman. Maybe other things'll come later."

Josiah said: "We'll fetch more supplies an' hay. We just come down to see how things was goin'."

Kingman spoke again. "I'll take the gray horse back an' leave the mare I rode down here on. She's quiet an. . . ."

"No mares!" Lane exclaimed

His partner looked steadily at Kingman. "We'll keep the gray . . . thanks all the same."

The older men declined an invitation to supper and rode back the way they had come. Reg said: "Why'd they come down here? We're doin' what's got to be done."

Jim Lee answered. "Keepin' you fellers goin' don't come out of their pockets. It comes from the church. Mister Kingman mainly'll want to be certain things're goin' well."

Lane had a question. "What do you think, Jim? Was he satisfied?"

Jim smiled and fidgeted. "I expect he's satisfied, but you can't never be sure with him."

Reg growled. "The hell with the son-of-a-bitch."

Jim visibly flinched. Mormons weren't great on profanity. It was doubtful that Jim Lee had ever heard a church bishop called a son-of-a-bitch before. Eventually he smiled, a trifle ruefully.

They spent the next three days hunting wild horses. The third day they found a small band, about ten or fifteen, mostly mares. One stud horse was alerted to them. His chin was as flat as a pancake, but he was a wild horse, age notwithstanding. Jim led off on a high and wide surround to get behind the band. The mustangs were heads-up alert, ready to run. The riders got so far westerly, the horses — not all, but some — went back to picking. Jim wigwagged with his upraised arm and disreputable old hat. They rode toward the horses, spread wide and at a walk. The old stud horse pawed once and snorted, the signal to run. The mares were slow responding.

Lane could see every detail. Mostly the mares were old, sunken over the eyes, a little gray up there, too. He wasn't close enough to see their chins. He didn't have to, and, in fact, he didn't get that close before the stud horse threw his head a couple of times and whirled to get his mares tracked.

The riders did not move out of a walk. Jim

came over to ride with Lane. He was grinning. Lane ignored him. He was watching the horses who widened the distance by the minute until they looked to be about the size of large dogs.

Jim said: "That's enough."

Reg joined them. He wasn't smiling as he looped his reins and methodically rolled and lighted a smoke.

Jim led off about three miles southward before turning in the way they had come. There was no sign, except a faint dust banner. Jim's little eyes were pinched nearly closed when he spoke. "They won't go much farther. They're mostly old. We don't head 'em any closer."

Lane was curious. "If they keep goin' in that direction?"

"Only water's at Lee's Ferry. They wouldn't go there to save their lives. Human smell."

"Maybe they'll go north?"

Jim shook his head. "Man smell up there, too."

"South?"

"Sure hope not."

They had the knoll in sight before Reg killed his smoke atop the saddle horn and looked at his partner. "We're goin' to be in the horse business."

Lane did not respond except to say: "Maybe."

The day was shot by the time they reached their camp on the far side of the knoll a fair distance, off-saddled, hobbled, and gathered around a tiny fire Jim built. Stachio hadn't ridden out. He was dozing in the shade, opened his eyes only long enough to see who the riders were, then closed them. He didn't come to life until Lane was frying tinned meat.

As they were eating, with dusk passing along toward night, Stachio said: "Some Indians scouted up the camp."

Lane spoke around a mouthful. "How many?"

"Six."

"What kind?"

Stachio raised his head. "I don't know."

Reg entered the discussion. "You're a native of this country. You're an Indian, an' you don't know?"

Stachio swabbed his tin plate until it shone before replying. "Many Indians down here. Hopi, Zuñi, Navajo." He pronounced it Nav-*ah*-ho the way the Mexicans and the Navajos themselves pronounced it. He put the tin plate aside, looked straight at Reg, and spoke again. "They hunt. Go long ways to hunt. No trouble."

50

The moon was rising when Jim went to the shrinking hay mound, gathered a healthy armful, and addressed Reg and Lane: "Bring along some more." He waited until they, also, had armloads, then led off on the lengthy hike to the encircled water hole.

Jim sprinkled hay mostly along the far curve, as distant from the entrance as he could get. Reg and Lane also scattered hay but closer to the thistles, ripgut, and buffalo grass westerly of the spring.

As they were walking back, Reg looked up. "That's a mighty skinny moon." It was a remark that required no comment.

Stachio was braiding wet rawhide. He didn't look up.

Reg walked out a way for a smoke. Lane joined him, after picking stickers from his shirt and britches. Reg offered the sack. Lane had his own makings. Reg said: "For a Mormon tame ape that grins all the time, he's pretty savvy."

Lane agreed, exhaled nearly white smoke, and gazed into the dark west. "You know how long we been down here?"

"No. Do you?"

Lane didn't, so he changed the subject. "Mister Stearn better bring more hay."

His partner nodded.

51

There was good graze in all directions. Hay was actually superfluous except that horses can't be worked on green feed.

Reg was stamping out his smoke when he said: "A sack of rolled barley would help."

They were listening to the deathless silence of a huge emptiness. When they were ready to go back, Lane said: "If it rained down here like up north. . . ."

"Rain? What's that? Partner, this is desert country, or mighty close to it. Lane, about those Indians . . . ?"

"It's up to them, not us."

"Stachio's an Indian. Why didn't he talk to 'em?"

Lane hung fire over a reply and came up with: "Maybe they aren't his kind of Indians."

They ended that discussion when they reached the little fire where Stachio was sitting like a Buddha, looking into the flames. He ignored them. They bedded down. Stachio hadn't moved. It was almost as though the dying little flame hypnotized him.

Mustanging was a variety of education. It wasn't exclusively the business of catching horses. People, too, were involved. Folks that sleep under the stars are commonly deep sleepers. Their blanket roll may smell powerfully of horse sweat, crushed under-brush, and bootless feet, but the days were long, the air was like glass, and folks slept like the dead.

This night was no exception until Jim Lee hissed and jiggled the partners awake. He was excited. The first thing Lane did, after sitting up, was rub his eyes and look for the horses. They were down there, sleeping hip-shot or picking.

Although the distance was considerable, Jim whispered hoarsely: "They're in the trap."

Lane yanked free of blankets, stood up, and stamped into his boots. His partner didn't waste time with boots. He uncoiled out of bedding like a striking rattler and started running to pull the ground cloth over its gate wire before the trapped animals could escape. He didn't make it. When Lane and Jim — who ran with toes inward — passed, Reg was sitting on the ground with one foot in his lap, rocking back and forth, groaning. He'd hit a round boulder with one foot.

Lane reached the trap, saw milling ani-mals at the water hole, and violently yanked the gate closed.

Jim came lumbering up, grinning from ear to ear. "We got 'em!" he exclaimed.

Lane was at the gate wire looking at their catch. It was a dark night. He turned slowly. "How'd you know they were in there?"

"I went out to pee an' heard 'em milling around."

Lane faced inward again. Some of the trapped animals faced him. He said softly: "Jim, you ever see a band of brockle-faced horses?"

Lee came to the gate, leaned, stepped back, and partially squatted. When he slowly arose, he was so chagrined he didn't smile. "Cattle?"

Lane's disgust was palpable. He yanked back the ground cloth on its wire, turned in silence, and started back.

When they reached the place where Reg was still holding his foot, Reg looked up. "How many?"

Lane delayed a reply. "What happened to you?"

Reg pointed. "That gawd-damned rock busted my foot. How many?"

"White-faced cattle," Lane replied. "Looks like maybe fifteen, twenty."

Reg let go of his injured foot and got onto all fours to rise. He made it but stood one-legged, his hand on Lane's shoulder as he looked at Jim Lee. "You Jack Mormon son-of-a-bitch, I'm goin' to slit your pouch an' pull your leg through it!"

Jim's reply was a jumbled apology and an excuse. He offered to help Reg get back to the camp and held out a big hand.

Reg struck the hand away with a balled fist, leaned on Lane, turned his back on Jim. "Walk, damn it. Slow. My gawd-damned foot's busted." Once, when they halted, he looked back at the big Mormon. "I'm goin' to kill you!" he exclaimed. "You half-wit son-of-a-bitch."

Jim brought up the rear all the way back to the camp. Lane almost felt sorry for him. He looked and acted like a little kid caught with his hand in the cookie jar.

CHAPTER FOUR
THE SECOND VISIT

By sunup Reg's big toe was half the size of an apple. He couldn't touch it, and, although he stood upright and walked a little, he kept the toe elevated, and he sat often. Reg smoked and was careful to let nothing touch his toe. Jim and the Indian rode out, seeking sign of the old stud horse and his harem. Lane rode out to the trap.

When Lane came back from the trap, Reg said: "That big, dumb bastard don't know the difference between a cow and a horse? I'm goin' to knock the whey out of him."

Lane sat in shade and shook his head. "He was tryin' to be helpful."

"Did you ever see cattle with their heads up like a horse?"

Lane let that go by. "He's good at what we're tryin' to do. He's run 'em before. Reg, why didn't you put your boots on?"

Bachelor was considering his swollen toe. "Don't know a cow from a horse. I'm goin' to. . . ."

"Leave him be," Lane said.

"Why, because he's bigger'n me? When

56

I'm through with him. . . ."

Lane rose, turned his back, and started walking. Reg sat a moment before calling him back. Lane returned, sat, and waited. Men who'd partnered got to know each other. Reg said: "I didn't have time to get into my boots. Besides, anyone knows the difference between cows 'n' horses."

Lane built and lighted a smoke, held out the sack, and Reg took it. The little, yellow strings of his own tobacco sack hung out of his pocket.

When Reg lighted up, he fixed Lane with a hostile look. "I'm still goin' to knock the whey out of him."

"He's pretty big and stout, Reg."

"Don't matter."

"Reg, he's like a little kid. I expect you can whip him, but it'll hurt his feelings more'n what you do to him." Lane killed his smoke. "Next time put your damned boots on."

Jim called from midway between the trap and the camp. He was pointing. A solitary rider was coming. The ridden horse had floppy reins and walked along with its head down.

Jim came back to the camp and joined the others, watching. He was first to speak and sounded astonished. "It's Pansy Dugan.

What's she doin' this far from home? Miz Dugan watches her like a hawk."

Lane raised his hat to make a crooked finger sweep through his hair. Reg looked at his bare, unattractive foot with the swollen toe. There was no way he could pull on a boot.

Jim walked out a way and called a greeting. If there was a response, the men at the camp couldn't hear it. The red-headed girl was uncomfortable. When she reined up, Jim said something. He was smiling. The girl made no move to dismount. She stole several furtive glances at the distant men, handed Jim something, and started to rein around.

Lane walked over. She let her mount stop moving as he said: "You're welcome to eat with us."

The girl looked away and back.

Lane's smile was genuine. He raised a hand to hold the cheek piece of her bridle. "My name's Lane. We met at the store."

She was looking at Jim, when she said — "I know." — and jutted her jaw. "You get the flank cinch. My ma said she'd take three dollars for it."

Lane dug out the crumpled greenbacks and held them up. Unavoidably their hands touched. Pansy Dugan briefly reddened.

The touch made a difference. She looked over Lane's head in the direction of the camp. "My uncle 'n' the others never had no luck catching them wild horses."

Lane grinned. "So far neither have we."

She looked down at him. "You will. Folks know about you being real mustangers."

Lane let that pass. Later he would ponder. No matter where a man was, there were folks who gossiped. He released the cheek piece. "We're glad your mother changed her mind about the cinch."

Pansy Dugan looked away again. "Her 'n' Missus Chancy went up to Saint George. They'll be back tomorrow."

Lane groped for ways to keep this conversation alive, but Pansy Dugan smiled shyly, reined around, and went back the way she had come.

Lane took the poop strap over and handed it to Reg. "Three dollars," he said.

Reg considered the **N. Porter** stamped leather. "She's sort of attractive, isn't she?"

Lane laughed. "We been down here too long."

Jim sidled up. He and the Indian intended to go tracking again. He looked steadily at Reg. "I should've seen that rock."

Reg looked up. "Maybe. Maybe I should've put my boots on. You and Stachio look out for those snoopin' Indians."

When Jim went back to where the Indian was sitting his saddle, he was smiling from ear to ear. There wouldn't be any fight, which saved things for Lane, too. He wouldn't have allowed it.

Reg mellowed. "How come her to ride over here?"

"Her mother went up to Saint George an' won't be back until tomorrow."

Reg stopped considering the cinch. "She's mindin' the store alone?"

Lane's answer was cryptic. "You can't put that foot in a stirrup, an' I'm not interested."

It became a hot, muggy day, the kind that preceded rain. There were huge white cloud galleons moving from east to southwest. Their progress would make a snail's pace seem like a horse race.

Jim and the Navajo returned with the sun halfway down, cared for their animals, and hiked to the camp to report that the old stud had taken his band south. Jim didn't sound pleased. Stachio said they'd watched some reservation jumpers from behind a pimple hill. They were poking along, reading sign of the mustangs. Reg swore. Lane was disappointed, too, but he said there were other bands.

Around the supper fire talk was desultory. Each of them had hoped the mustangs would be close enough to scent up the spring. The red-headed girl wasn't mentioned even though the new N. Porter cinch was on the ground beside Reg.

Reg limped to the trap to soak his foot in cool water. It looked like a half ripe plum, and, although the pain occurred only when Reg got careless, it seemed to Lane it was a tad less swollen.

Three of them went horse hunting the next two days. About the time they were ready to head back on the second day, Stachio raised an arm. The dust cloud was distant, but its source was unmistakable. Cattle didn't run; mustangs did.

Josiah Stearn arrived with a big shock of loose hay and two crates of supplies. He considered Reg's foot gravely. Todd Kingman was getting impatient for results. He told them Kingman had made up the difference for the flank cinch. He also told them Mrs. Dugan didn't want the mustangers around.

Josiah pulled a dour smile. "She won't let her girl anywhere near men."

Jim, Lane, and Stachio helped unload the horse feed. After the Mormon had departed, they did as Jim had done before, carried several armloads of hay to the trap.

The following morning Jim Lee was atop the little knoll that hid the camp and called. This time it was daylight. This time he didn't act hastily.

Reg limped up there with Lane. There were horses eating hay in the trap. Lane said: "Someone's saddle stock. They can see us and catch the scent. They're interested in the hay."

He was right. Even when the men walked in plain sight, the horses continued to scarf up hay. When they were at the gate opening, the horses stopped picking to regard the two-legged things. Jim pointed. "That's the bishop's mark."

There were four horses each with an old brand made of two large initials — T K on the left shoulder.

Reg dryly said: "Well, they do something right. Brand on the left side so's a man can't miss it when he mounts up."

The horses were uncared for animals with hoofs worn down near the quick. Two were recognizably old. The other two were younger but in poor condition. Lane wagged his head and turned to Jim. "Don't you people ever worm your critters?"

Jim simultaneously smiled and reddened. "I expect some do," he replied. "Want me to chouse 'em out before they eat all the hay?"

Lane, Stachio, and Jim got the horses out. Reg leaned on a crooked fagot, watching.

They were returning to the camp, when the sound of a very distant gunshot roiled the air. Stachio said: "Got one. Them Indians got one."

"Rabbit. Antelope maybe," Lane dryly said.

Stachio spoke. "Don't catch 'em. Shoot 'em. Cut off mane an' tail. Sell it at the trading post."

Lane and his partner were silent all the way back to the camp.

The following day Reg rode out, too, only one foot in a stirrup. The toe still looked like a ripe plum, but unless it got bumped, it wasn't painful. Stachio led. No one questioned his reason until near late afternoon when they found the dead horse. Its mane and tail had been shorn to the hide.

Stachio wanted to track the Indians. Lane vetoed the idea. If they found them, it would be awkward. If they didn't find them, it'd be a long ride back to camp.

Stachio didn't sulk, but neither was he talkative. He was never very windy. Over supper he opined that there would be no wild horses in any direction for miles. The sound of that gunshot would ensure that.

Lane was getting restless, and so, he thought, was Jim. On that score he was right. Lane, Jim, and the Indian left in the dark the following morning and were gone until dark. During their absence, both Stearn and Kingman visited. Kingman was blunt. He ignored Reg's foot. Josiah was tactful, but Todd Kingman didn't know the meaning of the word. He wanted to know when the mustangers were going to catch horses which was something no wild horse trapper could predict, and he annoyed Reg whose conversation directed at the large man was blunt and bordered on fight talk.

Kingman left the rest of the visit's conversation to the pale-eyed man, and Josiah Stearn seemed anxious to end it and head for home. After they departed and Lane returned with the others, Reg mentioned the visit. Lane shrugged. They had found a sizable band of horses that had come northward. It was a safe guess the band was one critter shy. It was also a safe gamble that the horses had fled northward after one of them had been shot.

Jim said: "We'll find 'em tomorrow."

Sometimes luck rode with a man. What they found was fresh sign of a band of maybe fifteen, coming north until they veered westerly. Lane told Jim he was getting the hang of this. The following day he and Jim Lee made a wide sashay northwesterly, well clear of the horse sign. What they found with the sun slanting off center was a mustang band headed up by a big, dappled stud horse. They sat their saddles in the distance. The stud horse caught no scent, and, because they were not moving, he caught no sighting, but from the possessive way he herded his band, it was obvious he was not only a stud horse but was young enough to be *coyote*.

They rode farther off, a mile or so, before bending around southward. The horses were not grazing along; they were picking in one place. After the gunshot that killed the mare, they had run their hearts out. This didn't mean they couldn't run again, only that running horses don't eat. This band was clearly hungry, otherwise they would have grazed along on the move.

Jim squinted his eyes nearly closed. It didn't help much. The sun was bright. He said — "I'll go south." — and rode away.

Lane waited until he thought Jim would be in place, then eased directly in the direction of the horses. The hungriest of them didn't see danger until the gray stud horse threw up his head and trumpeted. Within seconds the horses were racing easterly.

Lane rode slowly. He couldn't have caught them, if he'd wanted to. The best race horse on earth couldn't have caught up. Wild horses run free. Saddle horses carry a saddle with a man weighing maybe a hundred and sixty pounds.

Jim signaled with his hat. Lane saw and did not wave back. He assumed Jim was waving in exuberance because the mustangs were running in the right direction. Lane was not given to either exuberance or quick judgments. He was pretty much an even-tempered individual, the kind that made a good friend and a dangerous enemy. His principles were elemental. He despised liars and thieves and was loyal to the death, attributes which in later life would preclude the possibility of being wealthy.

The mustangs got far enough ahead to be visible only by their dust. Jim ambled northward until he and Lane were riding together. He was so tickled he could not repress it. He said: "We just might get 'em. They dassen't go south. Killin' that mare'll stick in their heads. Not the mare, the sound of a gunshot. They won't go yonder to the Lee's Ferry settlement. They might go north, but man-scent's up there." He triumphantly smiled at Lane. "We'll get 'em."

Lane nodded without speaking. It was a big country. Maybe other sources of water were few and distant, but they existed. The mustangs hadn't come near the trap despite the fact that according to the sign they had used the water hole many times.

When they reached camp, Reg was waiting. Stachio had gone south rabbit hunting. When the Navajo came back, Lane let Jim tell their story again. When Jim was finished, he looked at Lane, and Lane nodded.

Lane was hungry. Stachio got the fire going. The meal, as others, was sustaining but nothing else. Lane asked the Navajo if he'd seen anything during his hunt for brush rabbits.

Stachio answered without missing a mastication. He shook his head.

It did not require a Socrates to know that getting wild horses voluntarily between the wings of a trap was no sinecure. They had to be running, otherwise they'd notice when the wings narrowed to the gate and the trap. Jim did not have to explain this, but he mentioned hauling more cured hay down and sprinkling it inside, which they all did except Reg. His toe was almost down to normal, but it remained discolored. He had decided some days past nothing was broken. He no longer made menacing sounds toward Jim Lee, but that evening before they would try getting the horses into the trap he told his partner that there surely had to be an easier way to serve the Lord than catching wild horses. He was right, there were, but mustangers rarely knew what those ways were. It was also arguable whether they would readily give up running bronchos.

They bedded down except for Stachio. He sat, staring into the dying, little fire as he'd done before.

They were rigging out as the sun partly appeared off in the east when Stachio growled. A solitary rider was loping in their direction. Lane groaned aloud. Any other time . . . ! It was the red-headed girl. Lane speculated about Mormons' sleeping habits. An old man had told him one time the reason folks were early risers was because of their consciences.

She ignored the others, reined up a few feet from where Lane was getting ready to ride, and smiled broadly. Her other visit she'd been as nervous as a cat on a tin roof. This time she was different. She asked why they were rigging out so early. He countered by asking if she always got up before sunrise.

She reddened. "I wanted to ask you a question."

"Shoot."

"I saw you fellers smoke cigarettes." She pronounced it cigareets.

He nodded. She'd gotten up early to make the ride to ask that question? "Yes'm. It's a habit folks get. Me 'n' Reg smoked when we were kids."

"Isn't it bad for you? My ma says. . . ."

"Lots of things are bad for you. Far as I know, smoking's the least of 'em."

"The bishop said it's evil."

Lane hung fire over that one. "Maybe it is, for him. You folks don't drink coffee?"

"No, do you?"

"When we can get it. Smoke 'n' drink coffee. Sometimes whiskey an' beer. Pansy . . . ?"

She colored again. "Don't smoke get in your eyes? I like the smell, but. . . ."

The others swung astride.

Lane said: "We got to go. Someday, if you want, ride over an' we can talk more."

As he mounted, she asked: "How old are you?"

"Crowding twenty-two, Pansy." He smiled and reined around to join the others.

She sat back yonder, watching them go. The Indian was the last to pass. He gave her a wicked smile.

CHAPTER FIVE
CONSCIENCE

By the time they could see dust, the sun was climbing. Jim shook his head. The mustangs were heading south of the ferry settlement. They had to be thirsty, but they were avoiding settlements, isolated farms, and riders. He thought they should split up and ride wide. The idea was to get the horses running in the right direction. Some horses and particularly wild ones could be relied upon to race the wind. If a man saw them at all, it was by surprise, and that had to be pure accident. Barely keeping wild horses in sight was an achievement. Any idea of herding them was pure fantasy.

What they had to do was turn the band back northerly, then try getting them to sashay in the direction of the trap. There was no difficulty getting them heading northerly. The trick was to turn them, and Jim earned a merit. He got around them and wagged his hat and hollered. They turned. There was a good half mile between the horses and the big Mormon. Any closer and they would have scattered like birds. Later

Lane complimented Jim. Reg didn't. He said it was sheer luck.

Luck had something to do with it for a fact. The dappled leader made a beeline. Behind him the riders, not blinded by dust, would have prayed, if they'd thought of it or had known the process. The gray horse knew his direction. Westerly he and his band would be safe. Lane held his breath as the gray looked neither right nor left as he swept past the widest part of the wings heading straight for the trap. Jim whooped and eased his mount over into a run. Lane did the same. The stud horse did not stray. He had to see the fagot enclosure. He didn't even change leads. He led his band into the trap.

Jim reached the gate first, flung off, yanked the smelly ground cloth across the wire, and turned to remount. His Mormon horse was loping back the way he had come. Lane swerved to block the horse, caught one rein, and led the horse back. Jim forgot to say thank you. He was too embarrassed. Only women and children didn't keep hold of at least one rein.

The horses circled, bumped one another, struck the yielding, high fagots, and tested them, but not the gate where the men were standing. In the dust and excitement one horse, a runty, inbred six-hundred pounder, had gone wide and missed the wing. It never looked back, and for its size it was fast. It had reason to be. It was running in pure terror. Men had been killed getting in front of that kind of a horse.

Jim's exuberance intrigued Lane who had no idea the big Mormon was capable of that kind of excitement. Reg looked for something to sit on. His back was hurting. He had to settle for a leaning position at the fagots on the north curve of the trap. His reaction was in direct opposition to Jim's. He methodically rolled and lighted a smoke.

Jim took Stachio, went back to the hay pile, and picked as big a swath as he could. The Indian followed Jim's example. They returned to the trap. Some of the horses were wearing down. All were wringing wet with sweat even in the sunken places above their eyes. Jim and Stachio tossed the hay in, and that started the stampeding again, but this time, when the horses slackened, only a few still acted wild.

Lane said — "Give 'em an hour." — and went over to where his partner was also building a smoke.

Jim called over. "Eleven head."

He was wrong. There were nine, but dust as well as excitement and the possibility that

Lee's arithmetic wasn't the best created a situation where anyone could be mistaken. They remained at the tarp gate until the horses grabbed a little hay as they moved. Jim said he'd stay if the others were hungry.

Reg rode back. Stachio and Lane walked, leading their sweat-darkened horses. Stachio set the hobbles, dumped his gear, and went to search for something that would burn.

His horse knelt gingerly before rolling over and back three times. Reg made the horseman's comment. "Worth thirty dollars."

The horse couldn't spread its feet to spring up, so Lane went over, looped his belt about the animal's neck, knelt, and freed one hobble. The horse jumped up and shook like a dog, coming out of a creek. Lane rehobbled him, replaced his belt, slapped dust off, and went over into the shade.

Reg was gingerly trying on a boot. He didn't get far and cursed as he put the boot aside.

Stachio returned with dead wood sticks, dumped an armload, and said something about wood getting harder to find. As he was straightening up, he stared northward a long time before speaking. "Car coming."

Reg made no move to arise. Lane did. Sure enough a car was approaching. It was dusty but obviously a sturdy model.

Reg finally arose, limped closer to his companions, and said: "Preachers?"

He was simultaneously right and wrong. Where the car stopped, Josiah Stearn poked his head out. In the front were two aging, graying females. One of them also rolled down a window.

Stachio ignored the car, coaxed a little fire to life, put the pan of beans to heat, and used one soiled sleeve to mop sweat off and vigorously scratch his head.

Josiah Stearn asked if the ladies would like to get out and meet some genuine wild-horse hunters. Neither woman budged nor spoke. Josiah craned southward where dust was rising. He called out: "Catch a bunch, did you?"

Lane answered. "A small band. Jim says eleven head."

Josiah got out of the car, looking pleased. "The bishop'll like that."

Stachio was eating warmed over beans and potatoes from the fry pan. He had half turned but neither spoke nor more than cast one look in the direction of the car.

One of the women didn't raise her voice, when she spoke. She didn't have to. In the

Wolf Hole country spoken words carried. "Miriam, did you ever see such uncouth people?"

It was such an unexpected remark everyone but Stachio froze. He leaned, sifted a hand under an ancient cow pie, freed it from the grass, dumped some beans onto it, and began eating. One of the women made a sound of someone going to throw up. Her companion started the car, turned so tightly she ran over a boulder and several bushes. Josiah Stearn was just able to climb in.

Lane looked at the Indian. He would have bet six months' wages Stachio had never heard the word uncouth before.

Reg watched the Indian eating off the ancient cow pie and said: "Son-of-a-bitch!"

Back at the fire Stachio finished eating, tossed the ancient dung aside, and grinned. That startled the partners, too. Neither of them had ever seen him smile before.

Two days later Josiah Stearn rode down alone. The mustangers watched him care for his horse before coming over into the shade to squat and stare at Stachio. Eventually he said: "Why'd you do that?"

Stachio was expressionless. "Do what?"

"You know what . . . put them beans on that cow pie an' eat 'em off it."

Stachio's expression remained fixed. "Fry

pan was too hot. Tin plates not cleaned yet."

Stearn arose. "Where's Jimmy?"

"Down at the trap makin' sure the horses don't bust out."

As Josiah walked southward, Reg doubled over straining to control laughter. Stachio watched, expressionless as before. Lane wagged his head at the Indian. "Why, Stach?"

"Woman had mean voice."

Lane was satisfied. His conviction that the Navajo didn't know the word uncouth was vindicated.

Josiah came back. His expression was different. As he hunkered in shade, he said: "Nine head. Jim said one got away. The bishop'll like this."

Lane said: "Nine dollars worth?"

Stearn nodded: "I'll fetch the money, when we come for the horses."

Lane was curious. "What're you going to do with them?"

The answer shocked him. "Pick ones we can break an' shoot the others."

Stearn unwound up off the ground and pulled his saddle animal closer. As he swung astride, he said: "We'll rope the ones we want. We'll bring some riders to help."

Lane was quiet as he watched his partner divvy the hot beans. Granted the wild horses were inbred, mostly undersized from inbreeding, pretty much worthless, too small for a man and too wild for kids.

Reg interrupted the reverie. "Nine dollars. We can maybe catch more 'n' get enough money to get the hell out of Utah."

Neither of them knew they weren't in Utah. They were in northern Arizona. It didn't matter. They ate in silence. Stachio said he'd relieve Jim and left the camp.

Reg eyed his partner quizzically before speaking. "It sort of sticks in my craw, too, but we hired on to catch 'em, which we did. Lane, nine dollars won't get us far."

Lane looked up. "Shoot 'em . . . for chris' sake?"

Reg searched until he found a stiff, dead stalk of grass and went to work getting bean skins from his teeth. He interrupted this briefly to say: "It's no worse'n shooting them for their manes and tails."

Jim came back, and Reg handed him the fry pan with what remained of the beans. Jim didn't feel their mood. He ate, finished the beans, and plucked grass to swab the fry pan. Only when he'd done this to his satisfaction and put the fry pan aside, did he look at Reg and Lane. This time he didn't have to possess prescience; all he needed was instinct.

"Something's wrong?" he asked and got no answer, so he imitated Reg, found a dry sliver, and picked his teeth.

The Mormons arrived with the sun well up. Each of them had a booted carbine below and full saddlebags above. Todd Kingman rode on past in the direction of the trap. His companions stayed at the camp with Josiah Stearn who was palpably uncomfortable.

He introduced the four other Mormons. Two were friendly. One of the others shook hands without speaking or smiling. He was the eldest. The last Mormon was little more than a boy, freckled and shy, but he smiled as he shook hands.

Josiah said: "We'll wait until Todd gets back."

It wasn't much of a wait. The tall, large, expressionless Mormon bishop returned, sat his horse, considering the camp, and eventually groped in a pocket, counted out nine greenbacks, and held them out. Reg was hesitant. Lane asked a question. "You're goin' to turn them loose and shoot them on the run?"

Kingman put his steady eyes on Lane. "You got 'em. Here's your money. That ends it this time. Next time I'd like to see more'n nine."

Reg was reddening but kept silent, taking the money.

Lane said: "You didn't answer my question, Mister Kingman. What're you goin' to do with them?"

Kingman studied Lane, rubbed his jaw, and answered cryptically. "Keep the useful ones and shoot the others. Like I said, you catch 'em, we'll pay. That ends your concern."

Lane stated a fact. "You'd better have some real fast horses, Mister Kingman."

"We have. You boys can join the fun if you'd like."

Reg spoke sharply. "We got a different idea of what's fun."

Kingman put his attention on Jim Lee. "You go with us to clear the way."

Jim nodded and started walking. As the Mormons followed their bishop, only one nodded as he passed. That was the youngest one.

After the riders were gone, Reg said: "I'd almost give the nine dollars to yank that son-of-a-bitch off his horse."

Lane's sharp answer was prompted by what was going to happen. "You one-legged bastard . . . you couldn't pull a sick man out of bed."

Lane went into the shade. Reg limped

over to join him. The wait wasn't very long. The first gunshot sounded at least a half mile southward. For a spell there was no more shooting, not until a whole fusillade of gunshots sounded to the south, too distant to reach the men in the shade as more than faint, pop-gun echoes.

Reg handed Lane the nine crumpled greenbacks. "At least they killed 'em a long ways off."

Lane ignored both the offered money and the opportunity to reply. Not until the gunfire ended, the trap was empty, and all four mustangers were sitting by a stingy little fire did Lane speak. "They never meant to rope out some."

Stachio spoke for the first time — "Never meant to." — and left the camp with dusk strengthening along toward a half-moon night.

The horsemen evidently went back to wherever they had come from by a different route, because they did not appear at the camp.

Stachio rode out for the next three consecutive days. Only on the second day did he find dead horses southward, but on the third day, leaving ahead of sunup and not returning until after dark, did he find the others. The few southward had been stripped of manes and tails. The westerly dead horses had been worried by varmints, coyotes, and the like.

Jim Lee made a tactless remark that night at the supper fire. "Weren't no good, anyway."

Neither of the partners replied. They waited until Jim and Stachio went scouting before talking much. Lane said what he'd said before. The country was ugly, the people were mean, and just up and killing wild horses, using as an excuse because they grazed over country folks wanted for cattle, was a damned lie. "Cattle?" Lane snorted.

Reg agreed about the cattle. He'd seen cattle in better shape that were gummers.

Lane said: "How far will nine dollars get us?"

Reg had evidently pondered this because there was no hesitation when he replied. "Maybe down where that reservation is."

"We're not supposed to be down there."

"Well, we can go out an' around. Lane, nine dollars is shy of what we'll need. That gray horse needs shoeing. He walks like he's stepping on eggs. That's about a dollar, if we can find a place down yonder that sells shoes an' has a forge an' anvil to put 'em on."

Lane turned on his partner. "You want to

stay here 'n' catch more horses for those bastards to shoot?"

Reg pulled up his foot and was examining his toe when he answered. "You got us into this. You said we knew about trapping wild horses." Reg took some of the sting out of that statement by looking up and grinning. "You want to leave? We can head out tonight. I never stole a horse in my life, but I'll take the preacher's gray. For all I care that son-of-a-bitch can suck eggs."

Jim and Stachio returned late, cared for their horses, and came to the camp to get fed. A sack of beans cost one dollar. For men living out in the open and who weren't particular, beans were better than a snowbank. While the Indian was scarfing up beans like they were on the brink of extinction, Jim dropped his bombshell.

"Good-size band northwest. Big snorty sorrel stud horse is leader. We didn't spook 'em." When no one spoke, Jim wrinkled his forehead. "Somethin' wrong?"

Reg answered. "How many, Jim?"

"We was a mile 'n' more out. Maybe fifteen, eighteen head."

Lane's mood hadn't improved. "I hope you're better doin' sums this time than you were last time."

It was too dark to see Jim blush. He

cleared his throat, watched Lane build a cig-arette, and spoke again. "They most likely went west like the others did. Stach 'n' me figured the stink made 'em go that way."

Lane stubbed his smoke, went to his bedroll, kicked out of his boots, dropped his hat, and turned in, back to the fire.

Jim was concerned. "Is he sick, Reg?"

This time Bachelor hung fire before an-swering. "I guess he's sick. I don't feel real good myself."

Stachio spoke. "Beans all the time no good."

They bedded down.

Before dawn, when Reg sat up, Lane's blankets were flat. He groaned, tried one boot, then the other one. That one hurt but only while he was stamping into it. "Make breakfast," he said to Stachio, and walked in the direction of the trap.

Lane heard him coming, turned, watched Reg's stride, and said: "You're goin' to live after all."

Reg built a smoke and offered the mak-ings, which Lane refused. Reg lighted up before saying: "I don't give a damn, but, if we leave, we'd better wait until they're asleep."

Lane nodded. "You want the money. We'll stay. You're right. Nine dollars wouldn't get us far enough." He paused to face Reg. "But I'll tell you somethin'. If I never see Utah again, I'll be happy."

By the time they got back, Stachio had a fire going and the fry pan balancing on two rocks. Jim poured water sparingly. None of them was fond of packing water from the trap, the only water they knew of.

They rode out with Stachio riding point. Occasionally Jim corrected him about the route which the Indian ignored. His reason was sound. There was a series of rib-like, low bluffs. He led them far enough north to be invisible southward, turned eventually, and came in on the far side of the strung-out, low hill.

The horses were about a mile southward, grazing along except for a tall, breedy-looking bay stud horse with a wavy mane. He was after a mare who was only in her first day and fought him off. He persisted. She wouldn't take him until the second day of her heat, when she would have taken a cougar. Once he got close enough to nip her butt, and she kicked him in the chest. Fired up as he was, that hurt, so he left her alone long enough to lope in a circle to keep his band from drifting.

Reg said: "I'd like to get a better look." He didn't mean the stud horse. He meant the entire band. From a distance they looked slick.

Stachio said — "Long way back." — and that was the Gospel truth, a long day's ride back. He made another suggestion. "I ride double back with Reg. He turn the gray horse loose. If he can whip that bay, he know where home is."

Lane looked long at the unshorn, ragged Indian in silence. Turning the Kingman horse loose had no appeal. "That stud'll kill him."

Stachio continued squinting in the direction of the unsuspecting mustangs. "Maybe not. Gray horse will fight."

"A stud horse like that one!" Reg said.

Stachio didn't look around. He said: "Gray horse a ridgling."

Reg faintly scowled. He'd been riding the gray since the day they'd had their big jump. Ridglings pester mares until they come into heat. They also kick and bite geldings. They had stud instincts, and, in fact, some could cover mares, but ridglings shot blanks. They could not impregnate mares.

Reg twisted to look where the gray horse was standing hip-shot, dozing. He faced forward and looked at Stachio's back in silence until the Navajo said: "Jim, he get 'em closer."

Lee nodded. "Get 'em runnin' in the right direction until they're run out. It'd be closer but still a ways off."

They got astride, passed along toward the place where the landswell worried down to flat country, turned south until they could see the distant, dog-size wild horses, then Stachio reined up, looking at Reg. The gray horse and Reg had long since come to an understanding. Reg wouldn't put a cold blanket on his back, and he wouldn't try to fly.

Lane and Jim feigned disinterest. Both knew how a man and a particular horse formed a partnership. Neither of them had known the gray was a ridgling.

Reg dismounted, glaring at the Indian. "You get my horse chewed up, an' I'll lift your hair!"

CHAPTER SIX

HORSE FIGHT

Reg gripped the Indian's arm and swung up behind the cantle. Jim volunteered to carry the saddle, and Lane draped the bridle over his saddle horn.

Being free, the gray horse paused briefly before making a beeline for the wild band, and, before he got halfway, the wavy-maned stud saw him coming, pinned back his ears, and ran to the meeting.

The mustangers sat like stones. The stud horse reared high and came down to strike. He connected but glancingly. He lunged to bite. The gray horse swung clear.

The stud horse had a strong motivation. He would fight to the death to prevent an interloper from reaching his mares, and to the watching men the stud horse was obviously an experienced fighter. He settled briefly during a staring match, then walked forward. The ridgling was no novice. He backed and swerved before the stud could strike.

Reg said: "Go after the son-of-a-bitch, never mind side-steppin'. Wade into him."

The gray horse made a few lunges, but either had no heart for this or preferred avoiding the bay challenger, right up until the stud horse reared, curved, and bit hard as he came down. The gray was bloodied. Reg swore, but Lane, Stachio, and Jim remained silent.

Hurt, the gray horse whirled to flee. The bay horse came after him, ears pinned back, killing mad. Reg said: "He'll kill him." That appeared to be an excellent possibility. The bay was larger and longer-legged. The Kingman horse with blood running from near his withers down one leg made straight for the bunched-up band. He seemed to lose momentum. Reg was grinding his teeth. His horse was losing ground.

The bay was a neck's length behind, mouth open for another bite, when the gray planted all four hoofs, dropped his head, hunched his back, and kicked. Reg swore. He heard the gray connect with the bay horse's chest. The bay was solidly put together. Horses can't aim very well, but the bay horse staggered, veered slightly to be out of range, if there was another kick coming, and stopped still.

His band was getting restless. They weren't scattering, but they would. The gray horse went in among the wild band.

When the stud horse recovered, he came to renew the battle, but he'd learned about being directly behind the interloper, and he had been hurt. He'd lost some starch.

The gray horse rubbed against mustangs and left blood on them. They accepted him warily until the wavy-maned bay came to renew the fight, then they gave way. The gray faced around. The stud horse slowed down to a steady walk. He had to carry the fight to the gray. There were always studs willing to steal or fight for a band. The gray dropped his head and raised it, the gesture of challenge. The bay horse stopped. They looked steadily at one another, then the gray horse whirled, drove some of the band ahead, and ran for home.

The stud horse gave chase, but he moved heavily. That kick in the chest had done damage. He gave chase from pure spirit.

The mustangers moved out at a walk. Reg and Jim Lee would have made a run out of it except the distance was too great, and, as long as Reg's gray pushed his appropriated band in the right direction, little else mattered.

The gray had slightly more than half the band. The others went with the stud horse. Because he couldn't run hard, they set their gait to his, and eventually the distance widened between the two bands. Lane was hopeful but not very. Reg's gray might do what was wanted of him, but there was no guarantee. The gray wouldn't be the first broke horse that reverted nor would he be the last.

Lane tried a count and gave it up. Even the cut-offs with the stud horse bunched up, scattered, changed direction, until some were following but not keeping up. He made an estimation after four frustrated counts. "Eight head," he informed his companions and was instantly challenged by Jim Lee.

"Twelve head, not countin' them cut-offs with the stud."

Jim had been wrong before. In any case, until the mustangs were where they could be tallied, there was no point in starting an argument.

Reg was bleakly silent. His gray horse was tiring — and bleeding. There was an excellent chance the gray wouldn't sashay toward the trap. He was running arrow-straight. It was Jim Lee's opinion he was running blind. If so, he would keep going and bypass the farthest wing where they wanted him to turn.

Providence, or someone anyway, intervened. When the gray was far enough past the wings, he abruptly slammed down to a stiff-legged trot, head up, little ears pointing. There was a solitary rider ahead, maybe half to three-quarters of a mile. That was enough.

The horses with the gray slackened to a confused lope which eventually became a trot. They were about run out. The gray swung northerly. The others followed. He led them straight into the trap.

Someone whooped and broke over into a run. Lane followed. They reached the man-smelling tarp, neck and neck, piled off, and yanked the ground cloth closed. Reg dismounted on the wrong side to favor his foot. He ignored everything but the gray horse. It was bleeding. He went after his lass rope, waited until the circling horses passed, and snagged the gray which understood being roped and veered in the direction where the two-legged thing was taking up the slack. The others freed the gate and restrung it as the gray was led out.

Reg took the horse a short distance, then stopped to examine the injury which he didn't think had been made by a bite. It was too ragged for that. The bay stud horse had struck, not bitten.

The gray was sucking air and fidgeting. He looked ory-eyed. It was possible he'd never had to fight then run so far in his life. It would be a while before he came down to normal.

Lane walked back. He had made a count, and for a change Jim Lee had been right. "Twelve head," he told Reg, and leaned to examine the bloody place.

Jim and Stachio went after armloads of sweet-smelling meadow hay, returned, and did as they had done before, scattered it inside the trap, an action that brought the mustangs into another blind stampede, knocking each other to their knees, striking the fagots that yielded, then sprang back.

Jim and Stachio stayed at the gate. Reg and Lane led their tuckered animals back to camp. The gray followed like a lamb. Reg used precious hauled water to clean the injury. It wasn't as bad as it had originally looked, but the gray would be a while healing. The bay stallion's forefoot had torn the gray's shoulder. Even after it healed, the gray would favor that leg, not forever but for a long time.

Lane got a fire going, filled the fry pan with beans and onions, and looked around occasionally. Reg was babying the gray horse like a child. Lane went back to his chore. To real horsemen — not necessarily cowboys — an honest horse was a partner, not just something to be ridden.

Near dusk Lane went down to spell Jim from minding the gate. Stachio was chewing something and offered Lane a twisted, gnarled, lint-infested length of jerky about six, seven inches long. Lane accepted. Jerky had a particular benefit. It quelled the appetite. It also made thirst. The Indians had learned about jerky from the Mexicans who, in turn, had learned about it centuries earlier from the Moors out of Africa who had conquered Spain. They called it *charqui*.

Stachio said: "Many mares. Too bad stud horse got away."

Lane didn't respond at once. Jerky had a unique capability in that it absorbed saliva, and the longer a man chewed, the bigger it got. Finally he said: "I'm glad he got clear."

Stachio turned.

"Too good a horse to be shot, Stach."

The Indian neither agreed nor disagreed. He left Lane at the gate. He was hungry.

Someone had to stay at the trap during the night. It required two full days for the mustangs to settle, and even then, when a two-legged thing appeared, the horses would have another frenzy. But they stopped testing the wired fagots and by the fourth day would not go near the gate. They warily eyed the two-legged things with as much curiosity as fear. It helped, too, that

Jim and Stachio brought hay.

Reg doctored the gray horse. Ridgling or not, it got so it looked forward to being washed and handled. Since there was no way to pull the hide together and sew it, the horse would have quite a scar and possibly a sunken place, but the gray horse would never have won a beauty contest even before the injury.

Because the Indian and Jim Lee became familiar to the wild horses and because Reg more than likely wouldn't abandon the Kingman horse, Lane left camp early, riding north. He had no idea which house belonged to either Stearn or Kingman, but there weren't that many residences.

He found the right one when he saw an Indian, or whatever it was, duck around the side of the house at Lane's approach. When he stood with his animal and hollered — there was no hitch rail — the householder, who already knew who was out front, came to the porch. It was Todd Kingman, and, as was his custom, he showed no welcome.

Lane said: "We got twelve more, an', if you don't mind, I'd sure like a drink of water."

The big man's reply was brusque. "We got no drinkin' water, an' I'll be down tomorrow to look at the horses." Kingman closed the door after himself.

Lane swung astride to head back. Later in life, after he'd been to some god-awful places and had never been refused a drink of water, that was the one memory he had of Todd Kingman.

Something more important must have come up. Kingman did not appear the following day. Josiah Stearn did. He did not mention Kingman. He and Lane went down where Stachio was minding the gate. The mustangs watched but were more interested in scarfing up stalks of hay.

Josiah Stearn was studying the catch when he said — "I got your money." — and dug in a pocket.

Lane was curious. "Kingman told you how many there was?"

Stearn was counting out the greenbacks, when he answered. "No. All he said was that you got some." Stearn looked up as he passed over the money. "You know Pansy Dugan? She was ridin' over, saw what was goin' on, and turned back." Josiah Stearn neither lowered his eyes nor blinked.

Lane colored slightly. "We saw a rider far out. Good thing one was out there to turn the horses."

"You mind answerin' a question for me?"

"Maybe not."

"You boys real friendly with Pansy?"

Lane returned the older man's unwavering look. "Mister Stearn . . . not that it's any of your gawd-damned business . . . but no, we don't hardly even know her."

Josiah Stearn's expression changed. "Jim says you're decent enough fellers." Stearn paused to clear his throat. "Pansy's mother'd shoot whichever one of you she rode over to see some time back."

Lane said nothing. Pansy had said her mother had gone up to St. George and wouldn't be back until the following day. He made a tight, small smile at the older man. "You folks pretty good at spyin', are you?"

"No, not exactly, but you're strangers, an' we got reason to sort of look after our own."

Lane's temper was rising. He shoved the money in his pocket, looked up, and spoke. "I expect so, an' you shoot animals for the hell of it. Mister Stearn, you tell Mister Kingman that gray horse of his got hurt bringin' in those mustangs. I'll give him five dollars for the horse. To keep you bastards from shootin' him."

Josiah Stearn did not move as he watched Lane walk back to camp. He eventually mounted and headed back the way he had come. Before being converted, if anyone had called him a bastard, he would have done his best to bloody them.

Lane was still angry when he told Reg what had been said, gave him half the money, then told him the rest of it. Reg stuffed the greenbacks in a soiled shirt pocket, looking up from his shady place. "Maybe it's time to head south. We got plenty of money."

Lane nodded brusquely. "Leave the horses in the trap. I don't want to be around for another massacre."

It was late afternoon when they saw a solitary rider coming toward the camp from the east. Reg rolled and lighted a smoke and looked at his partner without speaking. Pansy Dugan was about ten yards away, when Lane walked out to meet her. It was getting along toward the hot time of year, so maybe it was sunburn, but whatever it was, she was faintly red-faced when she reined up and smiled.

"I didn't see the horses coming soon enough. Did I make you lose any?"

Lane shook his head. "I sort of wanted the leader to get away. Pansy, do you know what they do to those horses?"

"Shoot them?"

He considered her in silence, went to

work rolling and lighting a smoke without speaking.

She broke the silence. "I brought over two sacks of Durham tobacco."

She handed them down, and, as Lane took them, he smiled. "How much?"

"Nothin'. How do you make cigarettes?"

He said: "Get down. I'll show you."

She dismounted, standing close as Lane went to work rolling a smoke. Because he was already smoking, he offered the fresh one, and Pansy took it. He held the light. She took one draw and had a coughing fit. While wiping her eyes, she asked: "Do they . . . make you sick?"

"No. Try it again. This time real slow."

She obeyed, let the smoke trickle, and, although her eyes still watered, she smiled. "Smells good. I always liked the smell."

"Try again."

She did. He guided her along through several drags before telling her to inhale, which she also did, and immediately doubled over coughing and retching. Through bleary eyes she said: "Do you do that?"

"Takes practice to smoke, Pansy. You got to practice."

She coughed again with less force this time, and put the cigarette back in her mouth. She did as Lane had said. She drew smoke in more carefully. Nothing happened.

They stood out there, smoking, until she said she had to get back, mounted up, and sat a brief moment, regarding Lane, before she aimed easterly and loped away.

When Lane walked back, Reg said: "Her mother'll slit your pouch an' pull your leg through it."

Lane smiled and walked down to see what Stachio and Jim were up to. They were sound asleep in shade fifty feet from the gate. He kicked their boots. Stachio awakened instantly. For Jim it took longer. As he was rubbing his eyes, he said: "If they'd tried the gate, we'd've known it."

Lane was sarcastic. "Sure you would have."

He walked over to look in at the horses. They scarcely more than noticed him except for one old mare that had lost half of one ear in a fight. She walked up to the gate. Lane laughed. She was asking him when the next hay would arrive.

The following day, near high noon, Todd Kingman arrived. Because there was no horse holder, he led his animal up close. "How'd my gray horse get hurt?"

Reg jerked a thumb. "Over yonder." After Kingman walked away, Reg said: "If he don't sell the gray to me, I'm goin' to steal him."

Kingman returned and faced Reg. "Josiah said you'd give me five dollars for him."

Reg nodded, and Kingman held out a large hand. Reg fished for the money, counted it, and handed it over.

Kingman said: "You'll need a bill of sale."

Reg answered shortly. "No I won't."

Kingman changed the conversation. "That's a good catch. Next time I hope it's that good." Kingman paused. He evidently could not sense the antagonism. "We need fellers like you. Would you be interested in joining the . . . ?"

"Not on your gawd-damned life," Reg retorted, and rose to limp out where the hobbled saddle animals were picking. When he returned, Todd Kingman was gone. It would be the last time either of the partners would see him.

They rolled their bedrolls, waited until Jim and Stachio bedded down, then brought in their animals, rigged out, and headed south. Reg was leading the gray ridgling by a hand-fashioned, squaw bridle.

It was a warm night with stars like white freckles and a two-thirds moon. Behind them Stachio had not moved in his blankets as he watched them rig out and leave camp.

The following morning, when Jim asked questions, the Indian said he'd been asleep, had seen nothing. Someone had tucked two crumpled dollar bills in Stachio's hat lying near his bedroll.

The partners shared a stick of Stachio's jerky. Their animals plodded along on loose reins. Some scavenging coyotes, worrying a desiccated horse carcass with no mane or tail hair, fled like ghosts. They speculated about the reservation, decided to head more westerly, and keep watch. Indian police under whiteskin federal reservation agents were both eagle-eyed and very good trackers.

They came to a hogan beside a spring. The only water and the only hogan in sight, it was more isolated than they imagined. The horses needed water and rest. They headed for the inverted beehive Navajo house. Before they got close, an Indian came out, a tall, spare, older man, wearing the customary squash-blossom necklace and wide, sterling bow guards on both wrists. He smiled and raised one hand shoulder high in a welcoming gesture.

His name was Begay. There were more members of the Begay clan than a man could shake a stick at. He was called Hosteen Begay.

Lane hadn't recovered from something they'd encountered a few miles back. A dead sorrel mare with a baby colt. The little colt, maybe two weeks old, had walked in diminishing circles around its dead mother. It had nudged her, and toward the end of its life from starvation it had gotten down on both knees, trying to push a stiff hind leg clear to get at her bag. That's where it was lying, its head on her ribs when it died. The whole story was clear to anyone who'd ever read tracks. The colt's mane and tail were intact. It was soft fuzz and wouldn't be marketable for several months.

Lane's greeting to old Hosteen Begay was gruff. He would never forget that mare and her dead baby. Never.

CHAPTER SEVEN
AN UNEASY TIME

Hosteen Begay was a widower. Otherwise, the inside of his house wouldn't have smelled as it did and would have been cleaner. Old bachelors, red, white, or black, existed in the kind of squalor common to widowed or abandoned male critters. He ran a band of sheep, had a sorrel horse almost as old, relatively, as he was, and once had owned a dog. When the dog had disappeared, the old man had said two words: "Coyote pack."

He watched them hobble their horses from beneath a four-poled shelter of fair size with a thatch of underbrush. It got almighty hot, and summer was arriving. Inside, the house was dark, furnished with old Navajo rugs, some iron pots, a large *olla* for water, and beside some bedding on the floor near the back wall there was a corner stove of mud with a smoked-up front.

The old man spoke better English than might have been expected. He didn't say how he'd come by that ability, and neither of the partners asked. He stirred an iron pot with grease-watered mutton in it. Hospitality was important among the Navajos, and, when sheep became gummers, they ate them. The smell of cooking mutton required a particular kind of stomach, which was also required to eat mutton.

The old man was a blacksmith. Beneath his brush shelter a very old, large anvil was cross bound to a large wooden round. The forge was small. The tools were draped on nails. Reg and Lane had no difficulty settling in, and the old Indian seemed glad for their company. That was another thing about old bachelors: they need company. If it's not two-legged, they'll settle for tame varmints or dogs to talk and visit with. Hosteen Begay had no animals except for his band of sheep and the old horse.

After a supper of boiled mutton, which had Lane's stomach roiled with an urge to throw up, the old man brought forth a nearly empty quart bottle. It was *tizwin,* a very potent native kind of whiskey and tasted even worse than the mutton. It was forbidden on the reservation as were all varieties of liquor.

Lane sipped. On top of the mutton, the liquor made him excuse himself and leave the hogan. Reg smiled at the old Indian. "He pees a lot. Has ever since I've known him. We'd like to pay for you feedin' us."

Hosteen Begay refused, would hear no more on the subject, and showed Reg where they could bed down.

When Lane returned, he and Reg told the old man they were accustomed to sleeping in the open. Begay understood, went to watch bedrolls uncurled, sipped his *tizwin,* and, after they were alone, Reg asked why Lane had left supper. Lane's answer was brief. "To heave up that mutton. I never could stand even the smell of cooking mutton."

In the morning the old Indian was friendly but with an obvious hangover. He showed them his shoeing place, returned often to his house for water, and by afternoon, when they saw a horseman approaching, Begay was almost totally recovered. He watched the rider and said: "You hide in my house. That's an Indian policeman. He don't like whites on the reservation."

The partners went inside where their riding gear was, sat down, and listened. It was the first time either of them had heard the Navajo language. It seemed an impossible language to learn, although some whites had managed to do it. Lane, who had been born with an ability to pick up languages, shook his head. The conversation under the shoeing ramada was lengthy, but eventually the reservation policeman rode off, and the old man came inside, smiling. "He was looking for a Mexican named Higuera. He trades on the reservation. He makes beer. They try to catch him." The smile broadened. "Not very hard."

While Lane was returning from taking the horses farther out for better feed, he shot two prairie chickens. The old man and Reg heard distant gunfire and were anxious until Lane brought in his catch.

The following day two Indians brought in horses to be shod. Reservation horses were not shod until they got so tender-footed they couldn't be ridden. If there was an advantage to this, it was that the hoofs were too worn down to need much trimming.

The Indians nodded over the old man's introductions to the white-eyes, said very little, and hunkered under the ramada, watching the shoeing. Reg and Lane also watched. Old Begay made no extra motions. His little forge and ancient anvil were close enough to each other so that the old man had very little moving to do. He was obviously not only an experienced horseshoer, he was also very good at it.

He and the other Indians conversed in short, almost explosive sentences in their native language. Lane was sure the visitors were pumping the old man about the pair of strangers.

After they left on their freshly re-shod animals, the old man went to sit in the shade. He was drenched with sweat. His black eyes had muddy whites. He asked if either of the partners could shoe horses. They both could. The old man smiled. "You can help. Tomorrow comes the trader . . . Will Denver."

Clearly meeting a licensed reservation trader in territory where they were not supposed to be meant trouble. They discussed it. Reg was of the opinion that the worst consequence would result in being ordered off the reservation. Their excuse for being there was valid. While they had known the reservation was somewhere on their route of travel, they hadn't known where, exactly, the boundaries were. It was the truth.

The old man came out about dusk to visit. He was less anxious about their trespassing and the consequences than he was with having younger, muscled-up helpers under the ramada. He asked if they had money.

Reg said guardedly: "A little. Why?"

The old man considered the silver buttons on his moccasins as he answered. "The Mexican makes good beer an' sells it twenty cents a bottle." He looked up. "I show you how to find his *jacal*." He drew a map in the dust. "I give you money for three bottles."

It wouldn't be much of a ride over and back, but clearly the old man was sufficiently aged to have his share of aches and pains. Maybe someone else's share, too. As it would be this way, when visitors came, the trespassers would be gone. They wouldn't take his little, sun-face box half full of silver coins and left about sunup the following morning. There was always the chance they'd be seen, in which case the tribal policeman would return.

The Mexican was legally on the reservation and showed it. He was at least half *Dineh*. He was a jolly, narrow-eyed individual and offered three quart bottles for fifty cents each. Lane smiled and held out half that much. Higuera accepted the money, watched the bottles put into saddlebags, and in almost accentless English said that he would take it as a great favor that, if they were caught, they did not mention the name Higuera. He wasn't exactly a bootlegger. The Eighteenth Amendment to the Constitution had now been repealed, but beer was not supposed to have an alcoholic content of more than 3.2 percent. It was called "three point two" and was sold only by the quart. Small bottles and cans would come later.

When they got back to the hogan, the old man was sitting under his ramada with four other Indians. Lane was hesitant until the old man said: "These are part of my family. We've been waiting."

Reg handed the old man the bottles before going with Lane to hobble the horses. When they returned one bottle was empty, and the second one was being passed around. One of the visitors was young. Beer acted differently on Indians, especially younger ones. He waited until Reg and Lane had swallowed and passed the bottle along before saying: "You stole our land. You drive the people away. Many die on the long walk."

Reg recognized only that the young buck was antagonistic. He said nothing, but Lane did. He asked the Indian who the Navajos had stolen the land from, and that got a fighting retort. "*Dineh* owned the land before whites came."

Lane smiled tightly. "Maybe, but I'd say other Indians were here before you."

The buck jumped up. "You liar," he said.

As Lane got to his feet, one of the older men called an admonishment, but the young Indian with his share of beer lunged, fists pinwheeling. Lane ducked and side-stepped. As the buck came around, Lane hit him so hard he struck one of the ramada's uprights and bounced back. The next blow caught him squarely in the middle of the chest. He stopped, bent over, sucking air.

The older men arose, speaking sharply. The Navajo buck went off to one side. Hosteen Begay looked at the ground until the visitors finally went for their horses, mounted, and rode away. They had a brief conversation with Hosteen Begay before they left, and the old man leaned on his anvil after they were gone, clearly troubled. He said: "No good. It will be retold. They thanked you for the beer."

Reg nodded. "Time to ride on," he told the old man. "If we stay, you'll get in trouble."

Hosteen Begay's black eyes with their veiny whites showed a glimmer of hard humor. "You stay. Had no trouble in a long time. I like a little trouble."

In dancing shadows they picked over the bones of what remained of the sage hens. There was a smoke hole in the top of the roof, but in a mud hogan without a draft not much smoke went out the hole.

Shortly before they bedded down, the old man said the agent would track them down.

His last words were: "Stay. The trader will be here for horseshoeing."

They stayed but not comfortably. That beer taught them something they would never forget. Folks who didn't ordinarily drink, even beer as weak as it had been, could react as the young Navajo had reacted. Neither of them had any idea what that young Navajo's remark about the long walk meant, nor would they know for many years. The man who had driven the people away from their homeland was memorable among whites as a frontiersman, a national hero. To the People he was remembered, but not as a hero. His name was Kit Carson. What the young buck had said was true. Many Navajos had died on that long walk.

Lane told his partner, if they remained, it could only lead to trouble, for themselves and for the old Navajo. Reg did not argue, but oversleeping made an early departure impossible as did the arrival of a large, florid man, driving a top buggy with a sore-footed brown horse following, tied to the tailgate.

The trader was obviously not surprised to meet the old Indian's guests. He spoke with Hosteen Begay in Navajo, brought up his sore-footed horse, and tied him under the ramada's overhead boughs.

He was friendly, joked a little, studied the

pair of strangers, and watched the old man tie on his muleskin apron, fire up his forge, and study the sore-footed horse. It was not an old animal, rather slick as a mole, but clearly in pain. Begay walked over and handed Lane a farrier's knife.

Cowboy horseshoers were a dime a dozen. Genuine farriers were not. The old man watched Lane until he had rasped a forehoof and then went over, selected a cold shoe, took it to the forge. When it was hot, Hosteen Begay warped it over the edge of the anvil. The result was a pair of calks. He handed Lane the shoe, held by a long-handled nipper, and went back to his seat.

Lane dressed the hoof flat and even, fitted the shoe, which settled perfectly, and looked over his shoulder. The old man winked at him. After Lane had driven four nails to each side, cut them, clinched them, and rasped them smooth, he put the foot down and went to the old man.

"I never did any hot shoeing," he said.

The old Navajo got up, dusted off, and went with Lane to the offside hoof, raised it, and went to work. Not a word was said.

Hosteen Begay had been shoeing since about the time Lane was born. Every move or motion was precise and functional. When Lane asked a question, the old man would release the hoof, straighten up very slowly, and answer.

By the time the trader's horse was fresh shod all around, Hosteen Begay had made only a few comments, mostly about forge work. Shoeing was not hard unless a 'shoer made it that way, but it took its toll in injured backs. The old man had his own method of straightening up, one hand on each leg and slowly pushing until he was erect.

The trader paid his dollar, tied the sorrel to the buggy, climbed in, nodded all around, and drove off in a southeasterly direction.

Hosteen Begay watched. Southerly was the direction of the reservation's administrative headquarters.

Three more horsemen appeared with tender-footed horses. All were full-bloods, impassive, polite, and speechless except with Hosteen Begay. The old man did with Reg as he'd done with Lane, went through every step of the shoeing process from the forge to the final buffing.

No one noticed a visitor. Lane didn't see her until he went for the *olla*. She was sitting on an upended horseshoe keg. She was a little on the hefty side. Lane guessed her to be about twelve. When she smiled, she showed beautiful white teeth. Lane smiled back, returned to work, and, because it was hot, he shed his shirt. For some reason, possibly a *criolla* grandmother, he didn't sunburn. Oily skin cooked, got darker.

Hosteen saw the girl and ignored her. So did Reg. Her hair was shiny black and braided and hung down her back. Hosteen eventually said something in their language to which she gave a sharp answer. The old man resumed working, and ignored her again. The bucks who had brought the horses were mute and expressionless.

When Lane was working on the last horse, cradling a hind leg for nailing, a small insect hit him in the middle of the back. He paid no attention. He drove the last nail, when the same thing happened, a light touch on the back. He nipped nail ends, turned to balance the hoof on his leg, and went to rasping the clinched places.

It was the final touch and took maybe ten minutes. He straightened up, turned toward the *olla* for another drink, and something small hit him again in the middle of the back. He hoisted the *olla* to drink, and from the corner of his eye saw the sphinx-like bucks rise to dust off, pay, and bridle their horses. Hosteen was facing them. His expression was different. He was annoyed about something.

They rehung the pullers, nippers, farrier's knives, and rasps. When they faced around, the girl was nowhere in sight, and old Hosteen heaved a sigh.

Reg had been an observing bystander through most of the shoeing. He asked the old man a question. "Why'd she keep pitching those pebbles at Lane?"

Hosteen answered curtly. "She likes him."

Reg scowled. "Is that how you folks show you like someone?"

"No. Just girls. Let's go inside where it's cool."

Both mustangers poured water over their heads. It helped. It also wasted water that had to be brought by hand.

The old man got a fire going and put one of his cast-iron pots over it. This time there was no sickening mutton smell. In fact, after they had eaten, Lane complimented Hosteen Begay. "That was real good. No mutton for a change."

Dining was simple. A person rolled up a sleeve, and, when a piece of meat came boiling up, he grabbed it. The old man was wiping his hands. "You don't like mutton. I butchered a kid goat."

Before the partners finally left, a large

Navajo woman, a distant member of the Begay clan, came over to look in on the old man. She said something, and Hosteen's expression suggested the hefty woman did not visit often. She wore the customary squash-blossom necklace, massive turquoise bracelets, and a kind of business that kept her massive jet black hair away from her face.

She and Hosteen conversed in their native language. The little girl who had pitched stones was her daughter. Because her English was limited, Hosteen explained that, although the stranger with blue eyes and blond hair was welcome, she didn't want him returning her daughter's attention.

Lane assured the woman in English, which the old man interpreted, that while her daughter was very pretty — lie one — as a married man he had no interest. Lie two — neither of the partners was married.

The following day a solitary horseman appeared from the southeast. Hosteen pinched his eyes closed as he said — "Maybe agent." — and went out under the ramada to wait. His expression was strained until he was satisfied it was no one from the Window Rock country and called for Reg and Lane to come out.

The stranger wore a hat with a narrow brim, a shirt that once had been white, and black high-topped, English-style riding boots. He also held his reins in his right hand.

Reg said: "Where'd he come from?"

Neither Lane nor the old Indian answered.

When the stranger was within hailing distance, he raised his left hand — palm forward — as they'd told him to do back yonder. The old man returned the salute. As the stranger reined up, he looked steadily at the partners before dismounting at the old man's invitation. He held out the reins toward Hosteen. The old man masked his annoyance, led the horse into shade, and tied it there.

The stranger said his name was Henry Cleeve. He had heard at Window Rock, where he'd been told he could hire Navajo mustangers, that two *gringos* — his word, not the Navajo equivalent — were out at the Begay hogan. Maybe they were mustangers. The partners were to learn that Cleeve was a direct individual. He hadn't been successful hiring Navajo wild horse mustangers, when he explained the wild horses were in Mexico. Tomorrow would be his last day before heading back where he'd come from.

He asked if the partners knew anything about trapping wild horses.

Reg nodded his head without speaking, and Cleeve brightened. He had a contract with a company in lower California to supply them with wild horses, which the company made into dog and cat food. He would pay by the head — four dollars a horse, if Lane and Reg would accompany him the following day to northern Mexico. He would be in Window Rock, where he had left his automobile.

Reg jerked his head and, still without speaking, led Lane to the far side of the ramada, leaving the stranger and Hosteen Begay to pass the time anyway they could.

Reg said: "Four dollars a head?"

Lane's reply ignored that. "There's some gawd-awful rough country in Mexico."

"Lane, we were heading in that direction anyway. If it's too rough, we can just unhire ourselves."

"We got to have an understanding . . . we haven't seen the country."

"We can ride with him, leave in the morning."

And that is what they did.

CHAPTER EIGHT

SAINT TERESA, OUR LADY OF SORROWS

Reg led the gray horse. It was pretty well healed, but he led it anyway. It was hard to tell the old man they were leaving. He had taught them much. There had been the kind of bond forming which men understand and women do not. As they rode south, Hosteen Begay went under his ramada, leaned on the anvil, and watched until the partners were out of sight. Language made no difference; neither did reservation law. Old Hosteen Begay, without ever mentioning it, made the identical distinction Reg and Lane made. There are two kinds of people in the world: the kind they liked, and the kind they didn't like. Color, religion, language had nothing to do with it. In time, the partners might have learned the language of the People, but that was problematical, too. Lane, with an easy affinity, hadn't learned to pronounce a full sentence.

The partners angled in the direction of Window Rock where Henry Cleeve was waiting, and they found him with little effort. Automobiles were rare on the reservation, particularly ones with yellow and black license plates. Cleeve was in a restaurant, when they found him. He broke off his meal and joined them outside where he said that, although he liked mutton, where he came from folks skimmed off the grease.

Lane was less judgmental than Reg was. The longer they talked with Cleeve, the easier it was for Lane to accept him for what he seemed to be — a high-strung hustler. Reg took little part in the conversation, but he was careful to memorize the directions where he and Lane would meet Cleeve again, and it was a long ride.

They would learn that Cleeve rankled at any delay. When he suggested they sell their horses and go south with him in his Dodge car, Reg dug in his heels. He wasn't ready to part with his gray horse, and that's how the palaver ended, with Reg unyielding, Cleeve irritably impatient, and Lane siding with his partner. They were south of the Navajo settlement when Cleeve passed them in his car, waved, and left enough dust in his wake to cause a coughing fit in a brass monkey.

It was a considerable ride, almost the entire length of Arizona. Having money made traveling easier. They ate in villages, mostly Mexican fare, cared for their animals, and once had an interesting interlude with a Mexican-American policeman who was waiting when they emerged from an eatery. He wasn't unpleasant, just very professional. He wanted to know which of them owned the mule-nosed, pigeon-toed bay horse with Army numbers branded on its neck.

Lane said he owned the horse. The policeman asked to see a bill of sale. Lane didn't have one. The policeman asked questions. Horses wearing a US brand were not common among civilians. Lane explained how and where he'd bought the horse, in Wyoming at a surplus government sale. The policeman wanted to know if, when Lane had bought his mule-nosed horse, he hadn't been given some kind of paper to signify the transfer of ownership. Since the policeman had already been told Lane had no bill of sale and Lane explained for the second time, the policeman, a dark, 'breed-looking individual of some kind, grinned and held out his hand. Neither Lane nor Reg was acquainted with the Mexican custom called *la mordida*, meaning the bite. The policeman explained it to them. For a bribe he would forget he had ever seen either of them.

They gave him two dollars. He smiled broadly and departed. As Reg watched him go, he said: "This is Arizona, not Mexico."

Lane's reply was brief. "I've been down here before. The custom is to do what you can get away with."

The days were hot and dry. Water was important, more important than nearly anything else.

The little towns were almost totally Mexican. The closer they got to their destination, the more true this became. Somewhere back yonder Lane's mule-nosed horse had cast a shoe. The ground was like rock. It didn't take long for a hoof to wear down to the quick.

They entered a mud-wattle town called St. Teresa, Our Lady of Sorrows to find a smithy. Asking directions was useless. Answers came in Spanish until a tall, clean-looking, older man who spoke English directed them to the shoeing shed. His name was Antonio. That was his last name. His first name Joaquín. He even walked part way to make sure they found the blacksmith, a fat, short, raffish man with two gold teeth in front which inclined him to smile a lot. Gold teeth of such quality were symbols of financial well-being.

The blacksmith had been born in this border community. His English was good, if accented, and he was given to speaking in English and thinking in Spanish with some bizarre, even occasionally shocking English, as when the partners appeared at his dingy shop and, recognizing them as *norteamericanos,* he launched into English to impress the *gringos.* He said — "Of the bay horse of a certainty shoe him I will." — took the reins, and led Lane's horse inside his shop. He cross-tied the horse, cinched up his shoeing apron, and widely smiled. "I know what they charge up north. Fifty *centavos* a foot. By me, the charge is one dollar for all four feet." The blacksmith heaved both shoulders. "He is a good horse." He paused to squint at the numbers on the neck and went to work without another word. He thought: *If these* gringos *were riders of other people's horses . . . ?*

Two days later they met Cleeve whose anxiety — or impatience — was palpable. Cleeve had made what arrangements were available. He had rented a large, adobe-walled corral for their horses which didn't prove altogether satisfactory. The mud wall was too low. Possibly it had been erected to hold sheep or goats. Reg's gray horse jumped over into the next corral that held three mules.

The Mexican liveryman had a fit. The gray horse bit and chased his mules. He tied him out back to an ancient snubbing pole, hunted up the *gringos,* and with fierce gesticulations denounced the ridgling. They had to find another corral. This time it belonged to an old widow woman named Dorotea Saenz who was delighted to hire out her corral. Old widow women in Mexico who lacked large families ate poorly and rarely.

The countryside as far as a man could see, and farther, was desert or semi-desert. The partners rode out for three consecutive days, found barefoot horse sign aplenty. By the third day they learned from the squatty, congenial blacksmith, whose name was Albo Muchacho — meaning "white boy," although he was not very white and hadn't been a boy for many years. He explained the reason for so many barefoot horse tracks.

People rarely could afford to have their animals shod. The tender ones they simply turned loose and got another one with longer hoofs. For some reason known only to him he formed a warm acquaintance with the *gringos,* a characteristic not uncommon among Mexicans. They were good friends and bad enemies.

The village consisted of a handful of square houses made of adobe — dried mud. Its plaza had been created only God knew how long ago around a large well, walled to slightly more than knee-height to prevent dogs, children, and burros from falling in. There was a *cantina*, favored mostly by old men with skin as dark and wrinkled as old leather.

Reg and Lane settled in. Reg went regularly to salve the gray horse with mutton fat. Cleeve advanced them each ten dollars and was gone almost three weeks before his Dodge appeared and was admired by the villagers who saw few cars and in their wildest dreams could not imagine owning an *automóvil*.

Gringos were rich. It was known for a certainty that this was a fact. In a sense it was a close evaluation. One dollar was worth a pocketful of *pesos*. Silver dollars were common. If there was a disadvantage to Mexican silver coins, it was that, since they were pure silver, abrasion in pockets eventually wore away the handsome eagle sitting on a cactus with a snake in its beak. Counterfeiting was common. Some of the counterfeit coins were almost indistinguishable from ones that were genuine.

The blacksmith was blessed with a stout Indian wife and as many catch colts as she was unable to prevent being born. His woman raised a huge vegetable garden.

Their children, even the youngest and smallest, tended the crops with their mother, a seemingly stolid woman whose language her husband understood but others did not. It was a mixture of an Indian dialect sprinkled with what Spanish she had learned. Albo Muchacho was proud of his woman and his brood. He was immensely fertile. The children were visible proof of his manhood.

When Cleeve returned from wherever he went from time to time, he mentioned several natives who might help. They ran wild horses in their spare time. Reg and Lane were to learn they might have a great abundance of spare time but resented suggestions that they do anything they elected not to do.

Several miles northwest of the village of St. Teresa, Our Lady of Sorrows someone had once built a horse trap. Reg wagged his head. The nearest water was at least three miles distant, a huge, old trough of cemented stone fed by hollowed, small trees from an uphill spring several hundred yards distant.

They asked the blacksmith if anyone owned the land where the trough was located, and he rolled his eyes. "It is owned by *el patrón, Señor* Honorio Calderón y Macón who owns all the land for his cattle as far as you can see." The blacksmith paused to eye the partners shrewdly. "Not there," he said. "Never there. The *patrón*'s *vaqueros* shoot anyone. You understand?"

Reg said: "Not exactly."

Muchacho made vast gestures with both arms. "He raises many cattle. The places they water . . . no, *señores*. He will have you shot."

They mentioned the *patrón* to an old woman, sitting nearby on a bench in the shade. Her reaction was, first, to roll her eyes, second, to say in a rush of words neither partner understood that the *patrón*'s *vaqueros* had shot her husband years earlier for watering his horse at the stone trough. She crossed herself fervently, when she also told the *gringos* to be careful not even to ride on the *patrón*'s land. It would not be on her conscience. She had warned them, as, indeed, she had, although neither *gringo* understood anything she said.

In a small place word passed swiftly. By the day following the old woman's warning every soul in St. Teresa knew the *gringos* planned to invade the *patrón*'s land to catch *mesteños*. They rode out, farther each day, until they were satisfied that, if there was another watering hole for wild horses, it was not within several days' ride, if it existed at all.

Lane explained all this to Henry Cleeve, whose reaction was typical. "The land's not fenced."

Lane and Reg considered Cleeve. The only person who would make such a remark was not from open-range country.

Cleeve topped it off, when he said: "Ride out there. These Mexicans are impressed by Americans. He'll very likely be honored to let you trap horses on his land."

Cleeve also said he wanted horses soon. He had a contract with the Dr. Ross Dog and Cat Food Company over the border in San Diego. He had promised to deliver.

Lane was mildly annoyed. "You signed a contract without knowing there are mustangs down here?"

"No! There are wild horses. Hundreds of them. The company's been buying them from Mexicans for years. The trouble is the Mexicans are erratic suppliers. They can't run a company like that. They want a steady supply. Go talk to this Macón fellow."

His name wasn't Macón; it was Calderón. According to Mexican custom the last name belonged to the mother, the middle name, in this case Calderón, was the father's name and the only name to be commonly used.

The old woman they rented the corral from told them that, and forlornly shook her head. These *gringos* were going to get themselves killed, then what would she do for income?

They visited a mouse of a man whose shortness was at least in part the result of a humped back. Curvature of the spine was not common. The reason some were afflicted and others were not was known only to God whose ancient reticence had to be accepted. It was not a good idea to argue with Him, or to question the reasons He did things. Prayer was available, commonly through the priests and lay brothers whose standard explanation for every mishap left room for no argument. "It is God's will." This man's name was Jacobo Figuero. He owned a store that was not large and his trade did not warrant growing larger or increasing his inventory. Despite his humped back he was not a bitter man.

Lane said Jacobo Figuero reminded him of a spider who lived in a private web. It was apt. Jacobo Figuero rarely left his store which had only one window. It faced west. As a consequence his store was usually poorly lighted. The partners bought supplies. Jacobo Figuero was not surprised when they paid him in *gringo* money, but he was pleased and showed it.

Before the partners left, he invited them to have a glass of beer with him. Knowing no better, they accepted. Jacobo Figuero's beer was superior to most because he made it himself. They asked him about the rancher named Calderón.

"Why do you ask?"

They explained. The longer they talked, the more Jacobo Figuero's expression altered. He finally told them how the *patrón*'s men shot trespassers and reeled off names of the victims. He also said the *patrón* did not like *gringos*. When they mentioned riding out to see if they could use his spring to trap wild horses, Jacobo Figuero rolled his eyes.

"I'll tell you why there are so many *mesteños* . . . because they run over his land. I just told you. His riders shoot people."

Reg told Lane no one shot people just for paying them a visit. Because it also seemed unreasonable to him, Lane agreed. They decided to visit Honorio Calderón y Macón. First they asked the widow Saenz to describe him to them, which she did.

"He is a thin man. My father knew him, so you know he is old. He is mightily feared. His hair is almost white. He is light-skinned for a Mexican."

"You've seen him?"

The widow crossed herself. "I have seen him. He is the devil." She made a slightly imploring gesture. "You are young. Don't ride out there."

By the following day the villagers either avoided the partners or were kind to them, which was the custom to those soon to leave this earth. The days were hot; the nights were chilly. They borrowed a bucket from the widow Saenz and took an all-over bath behind Jacobo Figuero's store late in the evening. They cuffed their saddle animals, and Reg decided to ride the ridgling who carried himself well and seemed to have forgotten his wound, now almost totally healed.

Clean and fed, they saddled up. Reg had warmed the saddle blanket near a fire before cinching it. Lane watched. There was always the chance that a horse with a quirk would do it after he had not been ridden for a spell. The gray horse waited until Reg was ready with a deep seat and walked out like a tame old mare.

St. Teresa with neither electricity nor telephones had little excitement, but as the *gringos* rode north up the wide dusty roadway, the villagers watched discreetly, from ground doors or windows of their mud *chozas*. Figuero's store was crowded behind Jacobo's roadway window.

It was impossible not to notice. Reg said: "You ever been to Mexico before?"

Lane had, but no deeper than border towns which were different from the interior. "Not like this place. They act like we're not comin' back."

St. Teresa, Our Lady of Sorrows had two roadways. One passed through from north to south, the other, less marked and traveled, from west to east. It was the time of year when every footstep caused little puffs of dust to arise. They saw a large rock, clearly brought from elsewhere since in the St. Teresa country there were no rocks as large, and it had been somehow smoothed on one side where someone had chiseled out some adjoining lines and filled in the sunken places with a brand, typically Mexican. It didn't follow the *norteamericano* custom of straight lines. It had curves that created the likeness of three crosses, the middle one slightly higher and larger than the ones on each side. Lane speculated that it was an old brand. He had no idea how old. It had originally been the brand of Hernando Cortés, a Spaniard who was in equal parts hated by Mexicans and honored. He was the original *gachupín* — the first Spaniard.

CHAPTER NINE
THE VISITORS

There were cattle, small bands of them, grazing, some close, some distant, some so distant they looked to be ant-size. What interested the partners was that the cattle were predominantly longhorns, slab-sided critters with straight backbones. There were also Durham crosses, meatier built with small horns. The partners opined that *el patrón* had imported Durham cattle to cross with the Texas critters. Reg laughed. "At the rate this cross-breedin' is goin' on, it'll be ten generations before the longhorns are bred out."

The land had low swells, some kind of spiky brush with limbs like wire. There was buffalo grass along with other varieties of feed. It was reasonable to believe Texas cattle would thrive on the feed but not Durhams. Not very well, anyway.

They picked up the reverberations of mustangs on the run, but except for very distant dust they saw nothing to verify this.

Lane was curious. "Why would a cattleman protect wild horses?"

Reg looped his reins to build a smoke.

"I'm beginnin' to believe anything's possible in Mexico."

Lane did not reply. His partner's comment was close to the truth. Anything could happen, and, if a man waited long enough, it would.

They had been saddle-backing most of the morning before they saw rooftops, quite a few of them, in a setting of ancient and unkempt cottonwood trees.

Reg said: "Water, anyway."

Cottonwoods only grew where there was water.

They were concentrating on the distant buildings which looked to be maybe a mile or a mile and a half ahead. They heard nothing as they rode up a long, low land swell. When they topped it, someone let go with an awful yell. They reined to a dead stop. Reg hadn't brought along his six-shooter. The same idea crossed both their minds at the same time — *el patrón's vaqueros!*

On the downside of the land swell thornpin thickets flourished, some almost as tall as a mounted man. Reg said — "Son of a bitch!" — and started to rein around. If the *vaqueros* were well mounted, they could overtake his ridgling that was not built for speed.

Lane said: "Look, for chris' sake!"

It wasn't a *vaquero*. It was a solitary rider, seesawing the reins to stop a runaway mount. Both partners swung to make an interception, angling in the direction that would make this possible. Neither of them paid attention to the rider, not until they were only a few hundred yards ahead, blocking the runaway's blind route. It was a woman, black hair streaming, working the reins for all she was worth. It was a useless attempt. Her handsome, dark-golden horse had the bit in its teeth with its mouth closed.

Reg said it again, with greater feeling this time — "Son-of-a-bitch!" — and reined to be on the right side of the runaway. Lane spun to be on the left side.

They would have one chance. The dark-golden horse was running in blind terror. It leaped a low thornpin bush. Its rider lost the reins and locked both hands around the saddle horn. Reg had seconds to estimate speed and proximity. He led the runaway a few yards. Lane did the same on the left side.

The runaway stepped on one rein, broke it, and stumbled. Reg caught the unbroken rein in the air, rode beside the dark-golden horse, easing back a little at a time. On the left side Lane couldn't catch the other rein.

It had been broken only a foot or so below the bit, but he crowded the dark-golden horse, saw the white fear in the woman's face, and leaned to grab her and lift her free of the saddle. She wouldn't release her grip on the horn.

Lane felt his saddle turning, stamped hard on the off stirrup to get it straightened, and crowded the runaway toward his partner. Reg slackened pace for about a mile before the runaway responded. After that, the race continued for another half mile before the terrified horse could be stopped.

The woman didn't move. Her grip on the horn was like iron. She looked at her rescuers, when Lane told her to get down, which she did and leaned on the flank of Lane's horse, shaking like a leaf. Reg worried the runaway until it stopped fidgeting, then he sat there, alternately eyeing the handsome animal and the woman.

Lane spoke quietly to her, believing she did not understand a word he was saying. She looked at Reg, at her handsome horse, and turned her back as though she would be sick. She spoke in that position. "I've ridden her eight times."

Reg leaned, studying the sweat-drenched mare. When he straightened back, he said: "Snake bite, lady. Upper left leg."

The woman turned slowly. Her color was returning. She looked at the twin drops of blood. "I heard it," she said. "It was coiled at the base of a big bush. It was too late . . . the snake struck." She went to the dark-golden mare and gently ran a hand where the blood was and where a swelling was beginning to be noticeable.

Reg finally dismounted. The beautiful horse was sucking great gulps of air but was otherwise willing to stand while the people examined her.

The woman's English was flawless, no accent, no controverted words. She was not young, possibly her late thirties. She was solidly built, fair-complected, with jet black eyes and hair.

They helped her astride, rode on each side closely, and headed for the distant buildings. She said her name was Flor Calderón. She was the granddaughter of Honorio Calderón. Her parents had been killed in the wreck of a steam train back East. She was handsome in a mature way, and for some unfathomable reason she addressed Lane only occasionally, looking mostly at Reg.

The closer they got to the ranch yard with its old and sprawling buildings, its huge old trees, the more profusely she thanked the *gringos* for saving her life.

Reg dryly said: "She'd've run herself out, ma'am. Be a good idea if you had someone look after that snake bite."

She agreed. It would be done as soon as they reached the yard. After saying that, she was silent for a long time, looking straight ahead. As they were passing some mammoth, old, ragged cottonwood trees, she said: "My grand-father does not like *norteamericanos*. He is very old. His father was in the war against the *gringos* many years ago. You wait outside. I'll go in and tell him what happened."

She didn't have to tell Don Honorio. There were *vaqueros* on the verandah with him. They had witnessed what had happened. They were older men, but the individual between them was the oldest of the three. He eyed the *gringos* with a cold stare and interrupted his granddaughter when she started to explain.

He spoke English as well as she did but with an accent. He told the *vaqueros* to take the dark-golden mare and have someone named Fulgencio look after the snake bite. After the riders left, the old man offered no hospitality which, if the partners had known, was an unspeakable rudeness. He asked if the woman was injured, and, when

138

she shook her head, he told her in Spanish to go inside.

She went only as far as the place where he was standing. It was something he had been unable to become accustomed to, a woman who disobeyed and talked back. She said in English, "They saved my life. When the snake struck, I only heard it. Before I could. . . ."

"*Go inside!*"

She stepped in front of the old man and invited the *gringos* to dismount, which they did. "It will be time to eat shortly," she said, and finally obeyed. She entered the long, massive, old *hacienda*.

Her display of independence hadn't improved the old man's attitude. He said — "Wait. I will get you both five dollars." — and turned to enter the house.

Reg stopped him. "Mister, she don't owe us anythin'. Neither do you. It was a natural thing to do."

The old man had a knotty fist on the door knob, when he repeated it, only this time with the unmistakable tone of someone accustomed to being obeyed. *"You wait!"*

As soon as the *patrón* was inside, an elderly Mexican approached, wearing a soft smile. He spoke rapidly in Spanish, shook both the *gringos*' hands, and spoke again. He was weathered, dark, and lined. He was the *mayordomo*, what in other places would have been called the foreman, except that he had lived all his life on the Calderón ranch as had the other two *vaqueros*. It was the custom. A hundred years earlier, the big ranches held servitors in something like indenture. After a few generations the men and their families lived on the ranch, in their own way part of the world where the *patrón* was lord and master, also the godfather of the children. His name was Hermangildo Rosas. It required only moments for him to realize the *gringos* did not understand Spanish. He broadened the smile, nodded, and departed.

Reg watched him go. "He acted friendly, didn't he?"

"He was friendly. I think he was thankin' us for catchin' the woman's horse."

Reg sighed. "That old man is a sour son-of-a-bitch."

The old man returned with two ironed-flat U.S. five-dollar bills. He was clearly not going to argue as he pushed a bill into the hand of each partner. In his nearly flawless but accented English he said: "I warned her. It was her first time out, using a bit. She always rushes things. The mare was used to a hackamore."

Reg considered the old man. It wouldn't have made any difference if she'd been using a bear trap. He considered the money, the old man, and his partner.

Lane introduced them and waited. The old man made no attempt to return the courtesy. He was poised to turn his back and return to the house when someone called from the barn. The old man hesitated before walking in that direction without even a glance at the *gringos*.

Reg turned to mount. "Ungrateful old bastard. Let's head back."

He was ready to mount, when the handsome woman appeared. She said: "I owe you. If there is something I can do?" She ignored Lane, and Reg colored slightly as he answered. "Ma'am, we're mustangers. We came out to see if we could use that old water hole to catch some mustangs."

The woman was momentarily speechless. She glanced in the direction of the barn, when she answered. "My grand-father does not like *norteamericanos*." She had told them the same thing earlier.

Reg ran his reins through both hands. "He's not real friendly, for a fact," he said quietly. "Well, maybe there's another place."

She shook her head. "Not with water. Not

for many miles. There is a spring up near Rosario."

"How far, ma'am?"

"A hundred miles."

Reg smiled. "Thanks, anyway. It's been nice meeting you."

Flor Calderón waited until he was in the saddle before speaking again. "Wait. I will talk to him. Where are you staying?"

They were staying any place they unrolled their blankets. Lane said: "Near that old trough."

She nodded and disappeared inside the house.

On the ride back Reg said: "That old bastard."

"Yeah, but it's his land, his trough."

Reg shook his head. "A hundred miles, for chris' sake?"

As they passed down the wide, dusty roadway into the village, people stared. The consensus was that by now the partners would have been buried in some unmarked grave along with dozens of others it was rumored had met identical fates. When they were caring for their animals, the burly blacksmith appeared, widely smiling to show his pair of elegant gold teeth.

He addressed them as only good friends are addressed. "*Compañeros,* I worried. The whole village worried. Did you see *Señor Satán* . . . the old man Calderón?"

Lane answered. "Had a right nice visit with him an' his granddaughter Flor."

"Flor," he said and rolled his eyes. "Without a man all her life. It is a pity."

Neither partner agreed nor disagreed.

It was hot, nothing new in that part of Mexico. Their destination had been to warm weather where it didn't snow. The territory they were in had never seen snow, but it saw rain.

They ate at a hole-in-the-wall restaurant and swore they would never eat there again. The proprietor, more Indian than Mexican, laced everything with hot sauce, even breakfast.

They went to look after the horses. Rural Mexicans were not strong on haying. Their custom was to ride an animal thin then use another one.

They were cornered by the widow Saenz who had heard they had returned which signified that God was good, the *gringos* would still pay for the use of her corral.

She was more interested in Flor Calderón than in the old *patrón*. They told her what they knew, which wasn't much, and embroidered that with what they thought. The widow Saenz nodded her head from time to time and startled the pair of *mesteñeros* when she related that Flor Calderón and the old woman were friends. She explained that while meticulously examining a loose button. She and *el patrón* had once been close. Whether that meant congenially close or more than that she did not say. She also surprised the partners when she dug in an ancient locker, brought forth an aged six-gun with ivory handles, and offered it to them. It was the gun her husband should have been carrying the day he was killed.

Along toward dusk they took their bedrolls up near the big, leaky, old, stone trough. Reg said Flor Calderón would not appear. His partner said nothing.

She did appear, dressed in a *charro* suit, heavily embroidered against a background of soft leather. It was not attire women usually wore. *Charros* were leagues above *vaqueros* or *caballeros*. *Charros* were carefully selected by other *charros*. They were the elite horsemen of Mexico. Ordinarily they were wealthy. Commonly, too, they were descendants of original *gachupíns* long before the term was used derisively. She was riding a beautiful, chestnut horse with four white feet. She was clearly self-conscious, and Reg, never especially tactful, admired the chestnut horse.

Lane was a little more gracious. He hobbled her horse, removed the bridle and saddle, got her as relaxed as was possible, and asked if her grandfather had relented about the stone trough.

She sat on the ground and forced a wan smile. "He wouldn't listen. I told him we owed you that much. He said he would tell the riders to shoot you on sight."

Reg left off admiring her horse long enough to say: "It'd only be for . . . maybe . . . a few weeks."

"And then you will leave?"

"Yes'm. The man we work for wants as many horses as we can catch."

"He is a Mexican?"

"No, ma'am, a *gringo*. His name is Henry Cleeve."

In the poor light Lane noticed the slight change. "You know him?" he asked.

"No, but my grandfather knows him. While I was away at school in the East, he came to buy horses from my grand-father. He was run off our land."

Reg said: "Great. Lane, when Cleeve comes back, we better tell him it's not goin' to work."

The woman looked steadily at Reg. "You give up too easily. Give me time."

Reg answered that bluntly. "The old gent

145

hates *gringos*. He's had a run-in with Cleeve. Lady, we can't wait around. Cleeve wants horses as soon as we can get them, an' I don't think your grandfather's goin' to change. Why should he?"

Her answer was quick. "Because I am his only family."

Reg seemed poised to question her meaning when the chestnut horse nickered. Flor Calderón came up to her feet. Lane made a guess — a correct one — and said he'd rig up her horse. While he was gone, the handsome woman addressed Reg. "A week? Will you give me a week?"

Reg stood up, facing her. It was too dark to notice anything in either of their faces. He nodded. "If we can get Cleeve to wait that long. How will you do it?"

"I told you. I am all the family he has left. We are close. Have been since I was young."

Lane led up the handsome horse. Both men watched the woman swing astride, even up her reins, and boost the chestnut into an easy lope. They lost sight of her before they could no longer hear the loping.

Reg built and lighted a smoke. He said: "I got to shave in the morning."

They bedded down. Reg went to sleep without delay. Lane remained awake, listening to intermittent snores while looking straight up. Mexico's skies were clear, rarely cloudy unless rain impended. The stars were more brilliant than the stars of Wyoming or Colorado. He heard a slight rustling out where the horses were hobbled. It was impossible to move among the spiky underbrush without touching it.

In the morning three Mexicans were sitting on the ground. The partners recognized one, older, gray and grizzled with an expression which was not unkind. He was the *mayordomo,* Hermangildo Rosas. His companions were expressionless men with unreadable black eyes, and were younger. Spanish was an easy language to learn; a few days' association with Mexicans helped.

Reg stamped into his boots, regarded the three *vaqueros,* and sat down to rummage in his bedroll.

Lane spoke sharply: "Leave it be!"

Reg eased around, sitting close to the faint lump inside his blankets. The *mayordomo* spoke quietly, not without a hint of friendliness when he said: "You will saddle up and leave. You don't come back. *¿Comprende?*"

Lane nodded. The pair of riders slightly behind and on both sides of the *mayordomo* clearly knew little or no English. They were like stone carvings. Each had his holster tied to a leg. Lane had a question. "It is the *patrón*'s order?"

Hermangildo Rosas gave a slight nod of his head. He did not take his eyes off Lane. "*Sí*. Yes. Very soon. Today. And don't come back."

Lane hid a yawn behind an upraised hand. It required no great prescience. The old man had noticed his granddaughter's interest in Reg. The rest was easy. When she dressed all in black to be unseen, the old man had someone, probably the graying man opposite him on the ground, watching from the barn. After that, following by sound was all the Mexican had to do. Lane doubted that Flor Calderón had known she had been followed, out and back.

Except for agreeing to wait a few days, Reg had made it clear he was ready to leave, Cleeve or no Cleeve. He glanced at Lane in disgust.

The *vaqueros* got to their feet, their mission accomplished. As they went after their mounts, the *mayordomo* hesitated and spoke in English. "You saved her life. *El patrón* is grateful. *Adiós*."

Reg growled in the wake of the departing men. "They got a word for gratitude?" he asked, and began rolling his blankets.

A scorpion, half as large as a man's foot,

148

had been under the blankets for warmth. It came up with the blankets where Reg was kneeling to roll his gatherings. He didn't see it. He was listening to the *vaqueros*' loping back the way they had come. He put his hand squarely on the scorpion. Its normal reaction was to roll and strike with its tail. Reg's reaction was to rear back, knock the critter off, and swear at it. Lane took two long steps and came down hard with his left boot.

Reg had blood showing but very little of it. He looked up.

Lane said: "Get up. We got to find you a doctor. Those damned things got deadly poison." He knelt, examined the puncture, dug out his clasp knife, and made a deep slash. Reg didn't wince, not outwardly anyway. Lane used his belt to tie off his partner's arm above the elbow. As he was arising, he said it again. "Get up."

Reg arose and dusted off with his uninjured hand. "Where are we goin' to find a doctor around here?"

Lane ignored that. "Walk."

"All the way back to the village?"

Lane gave his partner a rough shove. "Walk! Shut up an' walk!"

The distance wasn't great, but to men accustomed to horsebacking it seemed long.

When they got down there, the sun was climbing and St. Teresa was going about its business before the heat came. After that the people sought shade behind mud walls three feet thick.

Jacobo, the storekeeper, took one look at Reg's swelling, bloody hand with its discoloration and told the partners to stay at his store. For a man with a marked curve to his spine the storekeeper moved very fast.

CHAPTER TEN
A CRISIS

When they entered the store, breathless and agitated, they put Lane in mind of a picture of witches he had seen as a child. Jacobo with his crab-like gait and the old woman behind him, hair flying, eyes narrowed to slits, attired in what had to be the cast-offs of others. Jacobo Figuero and Dorotea Saenz.

The old woman shouldered Jacobo aside, grabbed the bloody, swelling hand, and slitted her eyes nearly closed. Lane and Reg exchanged a look. Jacobo saw and correctly interpreted the look. He explained. "She is the *curandera*." Seeing that meant nothing, he said: "She cures people. And horses and dogs."

Reg looked at his hand, being held in the old woman's claws. He couldn't say it then, but later he could and did, when he told Lane, if that old witch was a doctor, he was going to die sure as hell. She sent Jacobo to find a chicken and bring it *andale pronto!*

She squeezed the hand, forcing blood out, but only a little came. The poison end of a scorpion is no larger than a needle. She looked up. Reg smiled. She shook her head and told him in Spanish to lie down. At his blank look she pointed to the floor and repeated it, this time in fractured English.

Reg looked at Lane who nodded. Reg got down flat on the floor.

Jacobo returned, holding an ancient chicken upside down by the legs. It was trying to twist free and squawked until the *curandera* took it, produced a wicked-bladed knife from somewhere among her clothing, and with one slash decapitated the chicken. Then she sank down beside Reg, disemboweled the bird, split it down the middle, and pushed the warm, gory body against the swelling on his hand.

Reg's face showed sweat. His color was increasing. Dorotea Saenz spoke rapidly in Spanish to Jacobo who scuttled from the store, closing the roadway door after himself. If it was his intention to close the door against customers, it didn't work. Two old men came in, stopped stone still, looked down at Reg. One said: "Holy Mother! At her age on the floor in plain sight with a *gringo!*" Then they both reversed themselves, closing the door behind as they left.

Lane squatted. Reg was sweating like a stud horse. He didn't respond, when Lane spoke to him. Dorotea Saenz held the splayed chicken tightly to the injured hand with her lips moving but producing no sound. Reg tried to free his hand. The old woman clung harder, using both knees on his forearm. Lane took his cue from her and helped hold his partner still. It was a mighty task.

Jacobo returned. This time he locked the roadway door. He said something to the old woman, speaking so rapidly the words ran together. He suggested whiskey. The old woman called him a bad name for such a suggestion but sent him for a bottle of beer, and, when it came, she told Jacobo to hold the chicken. When she was satisfied he had a good hold, she stepped to the counter, opened the bottle, and drank it herself.

Reg alternated between lucidity and something else. He was strong and determined. All three of them held him as still as possible. When the old woman removed the chicken, it had no drawing warmth left. She cast it aside and leaned close to study the swelling. As she leaned back, she addressed Lane in her peculiar variety of English. Jacobo interpreted. "She said he is at the height of the poison. Now we wait. He won't die but will be very sick."

Lane nodded. He had never been bitten by a scorpion but had encountered people who had. None had died that he knew of.

Someone rattled the roadway door. Jacobo ignored them. He, too, was sweating, but then almost any exertion caused him to sweat, and especially having a scorpion-bitten *gringo* on the floor of his store . . . !

Dorotea Saenz squeezed the hand several times with very little success. Even the fingers were swollen twice their normal size, and Reg vomited. Jacobo moaned. The smell would linger in his store. Dorotea Saenz called for rags and cleaned it up. As she was doing this, she looked at Lane and smiled. He interpreted that to mean vomiting after a scorpion bite was a good omen.

By late afternoon Jacobo's normal customers had stopped hammering on the door. Now they stood three deep, trying to peer inside, which was not entirely satisfactory since Jacobo's only window faced west and by late afternoon the sun was on the backs of the people out front, blocking its light. Reg was soaked with sweat. His face was flushed. He was clearly a very ill man.

Lane felt as useless as teats on a boar. He smoked one cigarette after another. When someone mentioned a priest, Lane thought that meant the end of a life was near. What it really meant to a predominantly Catholic people was that prayer would help hasten a recovery. It was a natural thing to ask but not very realistic. Priests only visited villages like St. Teresa, Our Lady of Sorrows on rare occasions. The nearest priest was a hundred miles northeast at the town of Rosario.

Dorotea, hair askew, sweaty, tired from exertion looked at Lane and smiled again. In Spanish she said the fever would break soon. He nodded without understanding, so Jacobo relayed it in English. To Lane it did not look like there would be improvement.

Reg was out of his head more often than not. Jacobo brought a pail of water and bathed Reg's face, an act of kindness by a person who knew nothing else to do. Outside someone squawked. Lane's attention was attracted to the scattering Mexican villagers. Two *vaqueros* pounded on the door. Jacobo scowled irritably, looked up, and had an abrupt change of expression. One of the men outside called loudly in a tone of voice unmistakably peremptory.

Jacobo scuttled to open the door. Lane recognized the *mayordomo* and a younger *vaquero*. Hermangildo Rosas shouldered Jacobo aside, stopped above Reg, and raised his eyes to Lane. He asked what it was?

Dorotea Saenz raised her head and spoke sharply. "*Escorpión* bit him. Look you."

The *mayordomo* leaned and slowly straightened. "We are to bring him back with us," he told the old woman.

She flared up. "How, on a horse? Are you blind, *estúpido?* He can't stand up. How can he sit on a horse?"

Lane asked where the *mayordomo* wanted to take his partner and got a reply that shocked everyone. "*El patrón* wants him at the ranch."

Reg had sweat running into his eyes. He was clearly possessed of a high fever. The widow Saenz wiped his eyes with a rag, and he blinked, fixed his gaze on the *mayordomo,* and said lucidly: "You son-of-a-bitch, what do you want now?"

Jacobo interpreted, omitting the first five words.

Rosas used English to answer, and Reg swore again. "You tell that old bastard I'm going to break his gawd-damned neck. I'm not goin' anywhere with you. *¿Comprende?*"

The *mayordomo* turned his gaze to Lane, who shrugged without speaking. The *mayordomo's* companion said they could commandeer the storekeeper's wagon, and Jacobo, who had been leaning on his counter, straightened up as much as he could. In English he said the *patrón* had told him years ago never to come onto his land. He never had, and his wagon was not going to, either.

The *mayordomo* addressed Lane again. "*Señorita* Flor has sent for the medicine man up at Rosario. She wants this one brought to the ranch. She will care for him."

Dorotea got up off her knees with difficulty and considered the *mayordomo*. "Where is Don Honorio, then?" she asked.

Hermangildo Rosas made a gesture with both arms. "I could hear them at the barn. I knew the *señorita* had a temper, but never like this. He yelled, and she yelled louder. He said some terrible things. She said they were all his fault. She will leave." Rosas turned to the *vaquero*. "Take the storekeeper's wagon. Jacobo, do you have a horse?"

"Why would anyone have a wagon and not a horse?"

"Go with him, Jacobo. I know what *el patrón* told you. We are old friends."

"Old, anyway," Jacobo stated sourly. "If he shoots my horse or destroys my wagon . . . ?"

"I will personally bring them back uninjured." To the *vaquero:* "Go! Jacobo go with him."

Dorotea Saenz went to rest against the counter. In the roadway people were milling, talking, gesturing. Neither Jacobo nor his companion responded to their questions. The *vaquero* roughly punched those who crowded too close.

Reg let go with a sharp yell and fainted. The old woman took over Jacobo's chore, knelt, and cooled Reg's face with the wet rag. When the wagon was out front, the *mayordomo* called on several strong men and led them inside.

Reg was now unconscious. They had little difficulty carrying him to the wagon. When Lane offered to help the old woman climb in, she stepped back, shaking her head. When he asked if she was worried about returning, because, if she was, he would bring her back, she answered — "I will never step inside that house." — and left them watching her walk away.

The *mayordomo* picked up the lines, his companion rode in back to keep an eye on Reg, who seemed still to be unconscious. Lane got his mule-nosed bay horse and followed. It fell to him to lead the Calderón horses.

Jacobo's wagon had no springs. The *mayordomo* drove carefully and without haste. Evening was settling. Night would follow but not for an hour or more.

Lane eased up beside the wagon. Reg was inert. He responded to every jerk and bump as though he were made of wet cloth. The *vaquero* made a small smile at Lane. For him this was a difficult situation. He would kill, if the *patrón* told him to, and the *patrón*'s aversion to *norteamericanos* was well known, but now the *vaquero* was involved in a mission of mercy of which he was positive the old man would not approve. As for the two *gringos*, the *vaquero* personally felt nothing. The one in the wagon with him looked more dead than alive and smelled. The *vaquero* knew about scorpion bites. People didn't die from them. They were sick for maybe a week, but they didn't die, and what sense did it make for this one near him to be taken to the house of the *patrón* who hated *gringos?*

There was a need for haste. The day was ending. On the other hand, for the *mayordomo* he needed visibility to avoid boulders, holes in the ground, those infernal bushes with the thorns. He watched Lane build and light a cigarette and asked if the *gringo* would make him one. Lane did. He even leaned from the saddle to hold the lighted match.

The older man smiled and said: "*Gracias.*"

There were lights in the middle distance. Candles made a weaker, yellowish brilliance. At the main house, despite the old man's aversion to innovation, there were coal-oil lamps that were better than candles. The light was brighter and whiter.

Don Honorio glared each time the Indian girl and his granddaughter went to the bedroom in the back of the house. He had adamantly refused the use of any other room, particularly the room in which his wife had died twenty-three years earlier. That room was kept immaculate. Nothing was moved. For the old man it was a sanctuary.

When someone shouted from the yard and appeared near the barn, holding aloft a coal-oil lamp, the old man went to the porch to watch the wagon enter the yard. It crossed over to the house, and the *mayordomo* climbed down, calling for help from the man at the barn before letting down the tailgate.

Getting Reg into the house was not especially difficult, but carrying him through the narrow bedroom door caused problems. The old man stood aside, his face set in granite. He would not look at the ill *gringo*, and, when his granddaughter hovered solicitously, he darkly glared. Lane handed the horses over to the *vaqueros* and was the last to enter the large, very old adobe house. He and the old man exchanged a look. Hostility was palpable.

Lane explained, and the old man cut him off. He had already heard from his granddaughter and the *mayordomo* all he had to know.

The handsome, sturdy woman came to the large parlor with its very old, very massive, dark furnishings and smiled at Lane. "Elena and I will care for him." She paused, her back to the old man who stood ramrod straight, fiercely obdurate and silent. "Elena knows about scorpion bites."

Lane raised his eyebrows. To his knowledge only the old man and his granddaughter lived in the house. She understood his look and explained. "Elena lives in the house with us. She cooks and cleans. She is a Pala Indian."

Flor Calderón turned with deliberate slowness to face her grandfather. He met her stare for seconds, then looked in the direction of a much-used, great, stone fireplace.

She addressed him in Spanish. "He is a guest."

The old man swung his black eyes to her face and said, also in Spanish: "He is a *norteamericano!*"

161

She and the old man had argued furiously about this. Her retort was fierce. "In your house, if he were the devil, you would show him the consideration of good manners!"

She left the parlor. The old man moved to face Lane who stood hat in hand. For a moment Lane expected to be denounced and braced himself. The old man went to a very old, very dark piece of furniture, lifted the top, removed two glasses, a bottle of dusty wine, closed the cabinet, and poured both glasses full. Without a word he crossed to Lane and held out one of the glasses. Lane took the glass and held it, waiting.

The old man raised his glass very slightly and said in English: "The first *gringo* in this house in a hundred years . . . may he recover."

Lane sipped the wine, and, although he was not fond of wine, this time the taste was neither sweet nor sour and went down the throat like water.

He thanked the old man, said he'd bed down in the barn, and got as far as the long, covered verandah before Don Honorio stopped him. They stood in almost complete darkness.

The old man said: "Tell me about this friend of yours."

Lane replied candidly. "We are the same

age. We've winter fed on ranches up north. It gets awful cold up there. We decided to come south. We trapped mustangs for some folks up near a place called Saint George."

"No! Is he married? Does he drink? Has he a temper?"

"He can get mad," Lane replied, thinking of the incident of the damaged toe and Jim Lee. "He doesn't drink any more'n I do. He's a good man, generous, honest. Why? You want to hire another rider?"

"No," Don Honorio replied with spirit. "You have been friends long?"

"Five, six years."

The old man fished forth a cheroot and lighted it. He stood, gazing across the dark yard where only one *choza* showed light. He aid abruptly: "It is my granddaughter."

"What about her?"

The old man showed temper. "Then are you blind as well as having been born with *ojos claros?*"

Lane bought time by rolling and lighting a cigarette. He thought about telling the old bastard Reg had a wife. Finally he answered truthfully. "What's wrong with them liking each other?"

The old man removed the cigar. "He is a *norteamericano!*"

"Is that a crime in your country? There's

plenty of *norteamericanos* who don't like Mexicans."

"They took half our country!"

At this point in Lane's life he knew very little about history. The Americans had fought a war with Mexico many years earlier which is about all he knew.

The old man misinterpreted his silence, swiveled the cigar to his opposite cheek, and spoke bitterly. "My grandfather was killed in the war between us. Flor's great-great grandfather. He would come out of his grave, if he knew how she looks at your friend."

Lane's temper was rising. "For chris' sake that was before either of us was born. Who did the Mexicans take their land from? The Indians?"

The old man said — "Another glass of wine." — and led the way indoors where distant voices were barely audible, and the parlor was empty.

He refilled the glasses, handed Lane one without looking at him, and led the way back to the porch. It was a warm night. The old man sipped. So did Lane. Neither of them had eaten lately. The old man gestured toward a homemade chair with leather backing. This time, when he fished forth a cheroot, he offered it to Lane, who had never mastered cigars but took it, and the don lighted it.

"She was very mad with me," Don Honorio said as though there had been no lapse in their earlier discussion. "She said she will leave. Go back among the Yankees where she went to school. She said some bad things to me, her only living family." Lane sipped, began to feel mellow, and relaxed without speaking until the old man said: "Why did you come here? Why didn't you catch wild horses somewhere else? Do you see what you have done?"

Lane smoked, watched the stars, became fully relaxed, and still said nothing.

Don Honorio sounded annoyed when next he spoke. "*Gringo*. I am ninety-three years old. Do you know what that means?"

Lane made a guess. He had known his share of oldsters. "It means you got aches and pains."

"No! . . . well, yes, that, too. It means, when I was young, we grew up with the stories of bad *norteamericanos*. Thieves, liars, killers, stealers of land. And now I have one in my house, and my granddaughter has turned against me. I raised her. I should not have sent her East to school. I was warned. Do you know that she came home with a big, wide place between us. And now this. . . ."

165

Lane finished his wine, shoved out his legs, and counted stars. Someday he would be old. Right now it was not a pleasant prospect. Who would he resent because they wouldn't approve of sending wild horses to a reduction works?

Don Honorio got up, wavered, and reached for the porch railing. Lane was at his side in a moment to steady the old man.

Don Honorio shook off the *gringo*'s stabilizing hand and did something Lane didn't expect. He smiled. "Listen carefully to me, *mesteñero*. I will give to each of you two hundred *norteamericano* dollars, if you will leave as soon as your friend can ride."

Lane said nothing as he half steered, half supported the old man to the door and inside to the parlor, where he left him.

Two hundred dollars each. Hell, they wouldn't catch that many horses in five years. He went to the barn, kicked some horse blankets to make a place to bed down, and was asleep almost before he got down on his improvised bed. *Two hundred dollars each!*

Lane was awakened by two chickens, one an elegant little rooster with black, curling tail feathers in pursuit of a small, harassed hen. The hen ran right over him. Her suitor had the decency to go around. They disappeared around a corner of the barn. Lane sat up, scratched, felt for his boots, stamped into them, and searched for a water trough.

The sun was coming. False dawn would precede it by about a half an hour. There was smoke rising straight up from the main house. It carried with it a tantalizing aroma of cooking. Lane hadn't eaten since the day before.

A *vaquero* entered from out front. He smiled as he said — *"Buenos días, yanqui."* — got a mumbled response, and went about his chores.

The trough was large, mortared stone, leaking as all such troughs did, and the water was cold. As Lane was drying off, the handsome chestnut horse with four white socks came up to regard him somberly before it drank.

Lane studied the horse. He had owned many horses but never one like this animal. It was slick, quiet, with a nice head, and good eyes. Maybe six, seven years old.

A voice brought Lane around. Hermangildo Rosas was smiling. He beckoned. They went to the small paddock where the dark-golden mare was favoring her snake-bitten leg. Someone had pitched in a flake of hay. She ate with no real appetite.

The *mayordomo* said in his horrendous English that he had shown the *señorita* how to break her horse.

The injured leg was swollen to the size of a baseball bat. The *mayordomo* shrugged. It was the same as saying the mare would be fine given time.

Someone called from the house. The *mayordomo* jerked his head for Lane to obey the call and left to do his own chores.

CHAPTER ELEVEN
BIG TROUBLE

Pala Indians are not tall and get fat early. Elena was no exception. Palas were normally friendly. Elena smiled at Lane before leading him to the dining room where Flor Calderón waited. Elena left. Flor smiled. She had put up her thick mane of black hair. It shone faintly as she said: "Ham and eggs? That's what Americans like back East."

He smiled. His stomach was making rude sounds. As they ate, he asked about her grandfather.

"He slept in. What did you two do last night? Drink his wine?"

"A little," Lane replied without looking up from his meal. "Is he all right?"

"By this afternoon. I've told him . . . a man his age shouldn't drink like a young man."

"Can I see Reg, ma'am?"

"Yes, of course. Tell me about him. He said things out of his head. Something about a red-headed girl."

Lane almost choked. "Up north . . . we taught her to smoke. Mormons don't believe in smokin'."

"She was special to him?"

"I taught her to smoke. Reg hardly even looked at her. It was a joke. Her folks don't believe in smokin'. They weren't real friendly. We got back by showing her how to smoke."

"Oh. Would you like more to eat?"

"No, thanks. I'm full as a tick." Lane pushed back to rise.

The handsome older woman also rose. She led the way to the bedroom. It had one tiny slit of a window, too small for anyone to climb through. What light there was came through that window.

Reg grinned. "How's my gray horse?"

"A damn' sight better'n you are."

"Maybe. I'm feelin' a lot better." Reg swung his gaze. "She's one hell of a fine nurse."

Flor went to the little window with her back to the men. Addressing no one in particular she said: *"¿Esposa?"*

The partners looked blank. She turned, color in her face. "A wife?"

Lane laughed. "Not me, ma'am. Maybe him."

Reg snorted. "Don't have one . . . don't want one."

Elena appeared in the doorway. There was a *gringo* outside. Flor left the room as

Reg said — "Cleeve, sure as hell." — and he was right.

There were now three *gringos* in the old man's house. Fortunately he was still sleeping. Lane didn't take Cleeve to the bedroom. In the parlor he said his partner had gotten bit by a scorpion.

Cleeve reddened. "How about the horses?"

Lane shrugged. Some Mexican customs brushed off easily. Until his partner was on his feet, Lane could promise nothing. He took Cleeve to the yard. "Come back next week. We'll know by then if we're going to get any mustangs or not."

Cleeve reddened for the second time. "They're out there. You're wild horse runners, and the dog food company up in San Diego isn't going to accept more excuses."

Lane nodded. "Next week," he said, and left Cleeve standing there.

Reg skewered Lane with a steady look as Lane returned to the bedroom. Flor Calderón had departed. Reg said: "Cleeve?"

"Yeah. I told him to come back next week."

Reg shook his head. "We're not goin' to have any horses next week, or next year. You should've told him he'd be better off to find another place an' a pair of different mustangers."

Lane said nothing. In the kitchen there was a softly audible lilt of someone speaking Spanish. Lane went out there.

Flor was with the old man who was eating sparingly of the breakfast Elena had prepared. He looked up. Lane expected an inquiry about Reg. Instead Don Honorio said: "Hermangildo went to Saint Teresa. They told him the *curandera* had treated your friend."

Lane nodded.

The old man squirmed around in his chair. "Do you know the old woman?"

"She's got a corral. We keep our horses there."

"That's all?"

"Yes."

The old man returned to his meal. He toyed with it a long moment, then mentioned Cleeve. Lane did not say he had told Cleeve to return. He told him Cleeve was upset that he and Reg had caught no horses.

The old man and his granddaughter exchanged a look. Flor smiled softly. Don Honorio sighed, rose, and jerked his head for Lane to follow. They left the house behind but stopped before reaching the barn. *El patrón* said: "You can make a trap.

There are too many *mesteños*. I protected them. They are wild things. Free things." He shrugged bony shoulders. "And then you both leave. Is it agreed?"

Lane nodded and extended his hand. The old man forced himself to seal the agreement with a handshake. As he was turning back in the direction of the house, he said: "Catch the horses and leave. Right away afterward."

Lane watched him reach the house and disappear inside. Later, he told his partner what the old man had said, and Reg wanted to leave the bed. Flor Calderón appeared in the doorway.

"One more day," she said, and moved toward the bed. Reg slid back beneath the blankets. She smiled. He smiled back.

It did not require a wise man to perceive what was passing between them.

Later in the day, when Flor Calderón came to care for her mare, Lane came up and said: "You talked him into it?"

Without straightening around she nodded. "He has said a thousand times the wild horses breed like rabbits."

Lane moved until they were almost facing one another. "Can I ask how you did it?"

She straightened up, looking at the mare's leg which was very swollen, but she could put her weight on it. "All you have to know is that you can catch the wild horses." She turned to pass back through the barn. The *mayordomo* appeared from nowhere. He said her grandfather had told him the *gringos* had his permission to trap mustangs.

She nodded and resumed her walk toward the main house. The *mayordomo* remained perfectly still. In all his years riding for the Trinity brand he had never imagined that the *patrón* would change his mind about wild horses, or *gringos*.

Lane saddled up and rode westerly. When he reached the area of the stone trough, a cloud of dust erupted. He stopped to watch the wild horses run. It was a fairly large band; he guessed about twenty head.

There were cattle out a way, clearly waiting for the horses to leave so they could drink. Leaky troughs made muddy ground which was good for hoofs in hot, dry country. It was also where wasps gathered dirt for nests, and they were unfriendly creatures. As Lane rode closer, the wasps came to meet him. He wouldn't know until years later that there was something about the smell of horse sweat that irritated wasps. He halted, swinging his hat several times, until the wasps left.

The ground for half an acre in the vicinity

of the old trough had been ground to fine dust by thirsty animals. He speculated about how long grazing critters had watered there. Probably before the trough had been built, and from its appearance he thought that had to have been several generations ago.

Mexican mustangs were little different from the ones up north. Maybe a tad smaller. Among mustangs there were only two kinds, studs and mares. Every nine months or thereabouts every mature mare foaled. The ones old Calderón had protected multiplied like flies. The gestation for cows was also about nine months, but bull calves were altered. It made a difference.

Lane rode in the wake of the dust at a steady walk. He had no intention of trying to get closer. He was satisfied there were several bands. On the ride back he looped his reins, built and lighted a smoke, and almost smiled. This time he and his partner would make money.

He veered in the direction of the village, found the golden-toothed blacksmith with the improbable name stoking his forge before going to work on a large, gaunt mule. Albo was pleased at the visit. He liked the *gringos,* but of equal importance, because they were considered a rarity, some of the awe rubbed off on him. Lane got the conversation worked around to a horse trap, and Albo's eyebrows went upward like a pair of caterpillars. He asked: "*El patrón* has consented?"

"Yes."

The burly man looked long at the ground before saying Don Honorio must be getting soft in the *cabeza*. It was common knowledge that he allowed no horse catchers on his land, as it was also common knowledge that he disliked *gringos* with a passion. Something was happening here.

Lane was interested in wood and wire, not what intrigued his friend. Albo said there were young men — not many, for most did not stay in the village — but there were some who would help erect the trap. He volunteered to recruit them himself. Such an action would impress people. Everyone knew the *patrón* despised *yanquis* and had allowed no trapping of wild horses on his land.

Lane was less interested in laborers than he was in the wherewithal to create a trap and wings. Albo said Jacobo had an abundance of wire. About the wood for uprights he was less positive. However, on the other hand, he was certain that for pay natives could be hired to gather what was needed.

On the ride back Lane got a surprise. Reg was coming toward him on the gray horse. When they met, Lane swung down. Reg remained in the saddle. He felt fine, he said, but weak.

Lane told him about the horses, the visit with Albo Muchacho, and Reg brightened. When Lane mentioned what he'd seen of the mustangs, his partner said: "Go tell the blacksmith to get his friends to commence gathering wood, haul it out near the trough, an' leave it."

Lane was willing. "We got to pay 'em."

Reg shrugged. Lane agreed to go back and make the arrangements. Reg watched him ride toward the village, reined northerly, and came out of a brushy cañon only to meet Flor Calderón at the far end, sitting without moving on that beautiful, white-socked chestnut horse.

Reg said: "You followed me?"

She laughed and jutted her chin upwards. She hadn't had to follow. All she'd had to do was ride atop the west rim of the cañon and watch. The view was uninterrupted for at least a hundred miles.

She rode into the shade, dismounted, and held the gray horse's curb strap. Reg dismounted a little awkwardly. He had an uncomfortable feeling. She was a very handsome woman, a tad on the abundant side, but as it was said of such women, shade in the summer, warmth in the winter.

As they faced each other, Reg glanced over her left shoulder. The *mayordomo* was motionless astride his horse, half hidden by a huge old thornpin bush. Flor followed Reg's line of sight, and exploded. She called to Rosas. Whatever she said must have upset him. He came into full sight and would have spoken, but she sprang astride, hooked the chestnut horse, and ran squarely at him.

At the very last moment he swung sideways. Their stirrups brushed. The *mayordomo* backed his mount, expecting another charge, but Flor Calderón neither turned nor looked back. She made a beeline for the yard.

Reg led the gray closer, and both men watched the chestnut lunge wide in a flinging run.

The *mayordomo* said: "Don Honorio . . . she will scalp him alive."

Reg toed in, used both hands, and hauled himself into the saddle. He endured the older man's steady look without acknowledging it or speaking. Flor was now small in the distance.

The older man mopped off sweat, pocketed the cloth, and spoke quietly. *"El patrón is coyote."* Rosas smiled. "He knew, when you rode out, she would saddle a horse."

"Something wrong with that?" Reg asked bleakly.

"In the eyes of her grandfather, yes, there is much wrong."

"Because the old bastard don't like *gringos?*"

Rosas shrugged lightly. "She is his only family. The others are all dead. He wants for her a husband. . . ."

"But not a *gringo!*"

Rosas shrugged again, made a rueful, small smile, and turned back the way he had come. Several hundred yards along he said: "We will not hurry."

Reg agreed in strong silence. He had no more wish to witness the fight between Flor and her grandfather than the *mayordomo* had.

When they had the big, old trees in sight, Rosas said: "I had children. It is not the same as when I was young. Don Honorio does not know how it is. Why should he? He goes nowhere. It is no longer possible for me or the *patrón* to pick those our children marry. You understand?"

"Yeah, *señor,* for a *gringo* I understand."

179

Reg said no more until they were entering the yard. He wagged his head. The differences between neighbors — his country and their country — was inconceivably vast.

A *vaquero* was cooling off the chestnut horse. It had been run too hard. If left to stand, particularly facing a wind, he would founder. The *mayordomo*'s expression hardened. He cursed in Spanish under his breath, veered off at the barn, leaving Reg to cross to the house.

Reg wasn't sure he wanted to. For a fact he wouldn't be welcome. He turned back toward the barn, almost reached the wide, door-less opening, when he was hailed from the porch of the house. The old man was leaning there, clutching the railing with white knuckles.

Reg left his horse with a rider and slowly paced his way to the porch. He didn't quite make it. The old man was angry, and because he thought in Spanish when he cursed Reg, furiously denouncing him, it was a jumble of words in two languages with a shrillness that made it impossible to make sense of. But the tone and the old man's fury were understandable, would be so in any language or no language.

In the barn the three Trinity riders didn't move. They seemed scarcely to be breathing.

Reg turned, walked back to the barn, rigged out his gray horse, and without looking in the direction of the house he loped out of the yard. He missed seeing Lane by a mile of brush, as Lane rode toward the yard. When he entered the barn to care for his animal, there was not a soul in sight.

It required no great amount of intuition to sense something. He was leaving the barn when the *mayordomo* appeared from out back and called.

Lane turned. The older man's voice was different as he explained what had happened. He neglected to mention his part in it. It would be a long time before Reg filled in the unmentioned parts.

Lane reached the porch at the same moment the door was flung violently open and Flor Calderón came out. She stopped stone still but only briefly before brushing past on her way to the barn. She was dressed for riding.

Lane watched her. He had to turn to do so. From within the house the old man said: "Come in. No, let her go. Come in!"

The old man was at the wine cupboard. His frailness was outlined by a streak of light from the window. With his back to Lane he said in Spanish: "Sit down!"

Lane sat. The old man brought him one of the wine-filled glasses. There was no salute. The old man held his glass, looking straight at Lane. "It would happen. You see? She has left. Drink your wine."

The old man half emptied his glass, went to the window, and stood looking out. "Three hundred years." He turned. "Three hundred years always with sons. Until now. In my lifetime. You understand?"

Lane sipped wine to avoid answering. He had no idea what the old man was talking about.

"*¿Gringo?*"

"Yes . . . *Sí.*"

"You are different from the other one. She rode to meet him. I knew she would. I want him never to come back. She said to me things I wouldn't say to a dog. And now she's gone out to find him. Do you know she is older than he is? Women get crazy."

The old man went to an elegant, small, carved, wooden table, opened a drawer, withdrew something, crossed to Lane, and held it out. It was a very old photograph of a young man, smiling as he stood beside a horse.

"You never knew him. That was Adolfo . . . my son. I had Hermangildo ride three horses almost to death to bring the priest

182

from Rosario. He died before he got here."

Lane handed back the photograph. "What did he die of?" he asked.

"The *vómito*." The old man returned the photograph to its drawer in the elegant little table, refilled his glass, offered the bottle, until Lane shook his head, then put it aside. "I would have had a son to keep the name. To make more family. And now even *she* is gone. To find her damned *gringo!*"

CHAPTER TWELVE
GETTING CLOSE

The next day Lane rode out. The atmosphere at the ranch made him uncomfortable. Flor hadn't returned. The horse she had ridden was not in the yard. Out of habit he rode in the direction of the stone trough and got a pleasant surprise. Albo Muchacho, he of the splendid gold teeth, was supervising two wagon loads of thick, rock-hard fagots.

He greeted Lane with a wide smile, gesturing in the direction of the two sweating young *peones*. They, too, grinned without pausing at their work.

Lane dismounted, considered the growing mound of wood, and asked the blacksmith how much he owed them.

Albo's smiled softened. "Three dollars. One for each of us. Is it enough?" It was more than enough. As Lane handed over three dollars, someone approaching from the direction of the village called ahead.

Reg had shaved, which was unusual. His trousers and shirt had been washed but not ironed. Even his black hat had been cleaned.

Lane went to meet him.

As Reg swung down, he said: "How did you manage that?"

Lane ignored the question. "Where is Flor?"

Reg's eyes widened. "Flor? At the ranch I expect."

"No. She left right after I got there. She and the old man had one hell of a fight. Over you. She stamped out, got a horse, and left. The old man is sure she went hunting for you."

Reg shrugged. "I haven't seen her."

Albo Muchacho came over, sweating and smiling. He wanted to know if more sticks would be needed. Lane shook his head. There were plenty, probably more than would be needed for a large trap. He asked about wire.

The blacksmith said he had spoken to Jacobo Figuero who said he had plenty and in fact for one *yanqui* dollar would himself deliver it to the trough.

After the blacksmith and his friends were on their way back to the village with two empty wagons, Lane thought they should have kept one of the men.

Reg took that personally. "You 'n' I can make it. We mostly did it up north."

They settled their animals in shade and

went to work. Reg tired easily, rested often. but otherwise worked hard. Without digging implements the best they could do was leave to the last what should have been done first. Thirst was a factor, so they quit early and rode to St. Teresa, got cool water from Jacobo's hanging *olla,* took him up on his offer to deliver the wire, and paid him in advance.

For the village of St. Teresa it was almost like *cinco de mayo.* Excitement was everywhere. It was unbelievable to the people that Don Honorio had permitted such a thing. It was unprecedented, inconceivable. At the *cantina* near the plaza nothing else was spoken of. A number of theories were advanced: The *gringos* had paid dearly in *norteamericano* dollars. No one accepted that. The *patrón* was a wealthy man. Someone slyly mentioned his granddaughter. It was said she was very fond of the blue-eyed *gringo* with the light hair.

The partners bedded down behind the smithy. Albo Muchacho said this was because he and they were close friends.

Lane hauled water to soften the ground where they would put the logs in the earth. When he returned, they got digging tools from the storekeeper — at half price. Jacobo had never liked the *patrón.*

They cared for their animals at the old woman's corral. She must not have been at home. Other times she had come out, sometimes to offer sweetened lemon juice which, it was said, was liked very much by *gringos*. It was her custom to fill one cup to the brim, the other cup not quite so full. She invariably gave the fullest cup to Lane. If either of the partners noticed this, it was not mentioned. But something else was noticed. The following morning at about sunrise, when they went to saddle up, the old woman was leaning in the doorway. She made no move to walk out as she usually had done. The reason was simple. While the animals were being rigged out, a younger woman, more robust, pushed past. Lane saw her first. Reg had his back to the house. Lane made a slight hissing sound, and Reg turned.

They were no more than fifteen feet apart when Flor Calderón said — "I apologize for my grandfather." — and made a tentative smile.

She was very handsome in her abundant way with the first daylight shining. Reg was clearly uncomfortable. "He's old, ma'am. Old folks got a right to be cranky."

"But the things he said to you!"

Reg grinned. He'd only caught one word

out of about ten. "He was fired up. Everyone gets mad now 'n' then."

"You are going out to the trough?"

"Yes'm."

"Would you mind if I came along?"

Reg looked at Lane who did what both partners were learning to do. Lane shrugged.

Dorotea Saenz came out. She had been married many years, and, it was said, there had been other interludes. She addressed Flor Calderón. "Come inside. Maybe later. They have work to do, and, besides. . . ."

Flor watched Reg and Lane ride away. The old woman wagged her head about something wild horses could not have dragged out of her before she would have put it into words.

It was the time of year when heat arrived early. This time the partners had a water bag along about a third of which they used softening more ground for posts. There was shade but precious little of it. They were resting in it, when one of the men who had driven a wagon the previous day came out astride a fair-size burro. It was the custom for riders of burros to sit well back on their rumps.

The native said his name was Pablo Gutiérrez. He would help create the catch pen for fifteen cents a day. Pablo Gutiérrez was in his thirties, powerfully built. Reg considered Lane, leaving the decision to his partner. They needed to keep every cent they had, but without another word Pablo Gutiérrez wheeled his burro and drummed on its sides. Burros were seldom fast, but this one went back the way he had come at a run close to setting a record.

Reg and Lane sat dumbfounded, watching. Pablo Gutiérrez neither looked back nor eased up the drumming he continued with his heels. Reg was disgusted. He dug out the makings and went to work, building a smoke. He had just licked it and was making the closure, when his partner said: "Look!"

It was a solitary horseman a considerable distance northeasterly. He was sitting like a statue. Neither the rider nor the horse moved.

Reg stood up, dusted his britches, doused the cigarette in the trough, ignored the distant watcher, and returned to work.

Lane said: "It's not the *mayordomo*. He would come on up."

Reg paused to lean on his shovel. "It's the old bastard . . . Calderón. I wish he would ride on up."

The motionless figure remained stationary for about ten minutes before turning back.

During one of Reg's rest periods, he said: "Want me to guess? He had second thoughts about lettin' us catch horses, got cold feet, an' went home."

By the third day they had the trap ready and worked on the wings. As that progressed, they eventually got too far apart to talk.

When things were finished, Reg told Lane to look after their animals. He was going to soak in the trough and come along later.

When Lane entered the Saenz corral, the old woman appeared with a full cup of tepid lemonade. He drank and handed the cup back. He could have drunk another three cups.

Dorotea Saenz wanted him to share supper with her. He weaseled out as best he could. His partner wasn't feeling well. She wanted him to bring Reg to her house. That required less imagination to weasel out of. Reg would sleep anywhere he went down.

The old woman said he needed an examination. By now he should be feeling much better.

Lane said he would try to bring his partner around the next day and left the old woman to walk until he found his partner.

Reg was two-thirds of the way back to the village, when Lane saw him. Reg was not alone. It didn't require the eyesight of an eagle to recognize whom he was with. Lane wondered how Flor Calderón had made the interception. It crossed his mind Reg would have been in a bad situation, if she'd come onto him, soaking naked in the trough. They hadn't met like that, but it was close. Flor Calderón had told Reg that Cleeve was looking for him. As Lane walked up, she was explaining that she had told Cleeve the trap was almost finished, that his mustangers would have horses for him in a few days.

Cleeve had asked Flor Calderón to tell Lane and Reg unless they had horses for him by the following week he would find other mustangers — and they could return the ten dollars he had advanced them.

Lane listened, nodded, and left it up to his partner to explain to the handsome woman how they were involved with Cleeve and walked into shade and waited because, clearly, he was the fifth wheel while those two were talking.

When Flor Calderón mounted the chestnut with four white stockings and departed, Reg came over into the shade and sank down. "We came here to run mustangs."

Lane nodded. That statement was indisputable.

Reg turned. "We're mixed up in a gawd-damned family mess. She told me the old man wants to talk to you."

"Me? What'n hell does he want to talk to me about?"

"She didn't say. Maybe she doesn't know. All she said was that the old bastard wants to talk to you."

Lane stood up, dusted off, and jerked his head. On their way to St. Teresa he was uneasy. When they were entering the village, he said: "Let's hurry this up. As long as man smell is back there, the horses won't come to drink. By tomorrow evenin' let's see if they've come, an', if they did, let's get set up to catch 'em day after tomorrow."

Reg looked at Lane. "No damned cattle this time."

They both laughed.

The following morning Cleeve caught up with them in his Dodge car, which looked as though it had been overtaken by a massive duststorm. He had seen the trap which was probably what made his mood almost uncomfortably effusive. He said by the middle of the ensuing week the rendering company over the line in San Diego would cancel his contract. Reg and Lane were sure they could have horses for him before then.

Lane was curious. "How do you get them from the trap to San Diego?"

Cleeve was almost condescending when he answered. "By truck to the railroad. By train from there to the company's corrals." He paused. "Do you know what hoof-and-mouth disease is?"

They knew. The Mexicans called it *aftosa*. If they made an effort to control it, the *norteamericanos* were not impressed with their effort, so wild horses brought over the line had to be branded D on the cheek, and, when they were loaded in cattle cars, the cars were locked and sealed. The letter D signified the horses were to be destroyed. There would be *gringo* inspectors at the San Diego end of the trip to break the seals and unlock the cars.

Reg said: "Brand 'em? Who's going to do that? Those sons-of-bitches are wild. They'll fight like a buzz saw."

Cleeve's reply was reassuring. "I've hired some Texans to do the marking before the train crosses out of Mexico."

Reg shook his head.

After Cleeve left, the partners rode a wide surround of the territory. They didn't see a wild horse, but they saw plenty of dust. The mustangs hadn't been able to get to water for several days. Lane did not mention his thoughts. He was almost convinced their work was going to pay off. The question in his mind was how many horses they could trap.

Jacobo, the storekeeper, took them to a café twice as long as it was wide. The place was empty when they entered. Jacobo and the massively bewhiskered proprietor exchanged a few words.

The caféman brought them beer. He knew so little English he spoke only to Jacobo. The beer was warm and gritty, but, having had no beer in a long time, the partners emptied their glasses and called for refills.

When the meal arrived, it was a surprise. There were no refried beans, a staple, and the steaks had been marinated in a reddish sauce, thick as molasses. Jacobo ate a side dish so powerfully laced with garlic the aroma almost made the *gringos'* eyes water. They were finishing the meal, when Albo Muchacho walked in. He had, he said, been looking for the partners. He had heard the trap was ready and offered to help with several friends to go far out and drift the mustangs in the direction of the trap.

Lane was grateful, but, because the mustangs hadn't had water in several hot days, he didn't think outriders would be needed, and, in fact, mounted men, no matter how *coyote* they might be, would be scented and the wild horses would scatter in all directions. They offered to stand the blacksmith a beer. He accepted and drank two bottles before slapping Lane on the shoulder and departing. He hadn't really wanted to do all that horsebacking in the heat anyway.

Lane went to look in on their horses. The gray was menacing a tall mule over the fence, ears pulled back, slashing with his teeth. The big mule stood clear without showing fear.

Dorotea Saenz appeared with a cup of lemonade. As Lane was drinking, she asked: "You will catch the horses?"

He nodded until he'd swallowed, handed back the cup, and smiled. "I think so. Why? Do you want us to cut one out for you?"

The old woman looked dismayed. "I couldn't feed it. Wild horses belong wild. Where is your friend?"

"Bedding down. He gets tired easy. But he'll be all right."

"He should stay here until he's recovered. I have a spare room." The old woman's gaze was stone steady. "I know how Don Honorio talked to him. He is a person without a soul."

Lane leaned on the adobe wall, considering the gray horse. Reg was fond of that animal. How could they get him out of Mexico?

Dorotea Saenz ignored the gray horse. "There is a man who can get your horses out of Mexico without trouble at the border. He would charge twenty-five cents a head."

Lane turned. "You mean smuggle them over the line?"

"Yes. His name is. . . ."

"Ma'am, getting them over the line won't cost us anything. That's the business of the feller we hand 'em over to."

The old woman reverted to an earlier subject. "If your friend would wait a few days . . . let me look after the scorpion bite . . . it would be better."

Reg was fully recovered except for having to rest often, and Lane wasn't convinced that was the result of the bite but from lying in bed. "I'll talk to him," he said, smiled, and left the old woman, looking after him.

The following morning Reg was stirring in the dark. He wanted to get this job finished. He and Lane returned to the café of the bearded man who greeted them with a nod but without speaking. There were three other diners. One was eating fried eggs and potatoes. The partners pointed and nodded.

Dawn was breaking. Reg was anxious. As they left the village in the direction of the trap, some villagers watched. *Huarache* telegraph was more reliable than the other kind.

Mustangs and cattle had both been at the trough. Based on the sign, the cattle had showed less concern about the trap and its wings than the wild horses had. The horses had clearly milled, some had missed the wings, others had gulped water before fleeing.

Reg tried to estimate how many horses from tracks but gave it up. Too many cattle had stirred the same dust.

They rigged the ground-cloth gate, rode back to the village, and encountered Cleeve. He was talking to Flor Calderón out front of the Saenz residence.

When he saw them, he left the handsome woman, made an interception, and, as they were dismounting, he hastened up. "Everybody in this place knows what you've been doing. Will they enter your trap?"

Reg, whose patience with Cleeve had been wearing thin for some time, said: "There's always a chance. Only wild horses aren't reliable."

Cleeve's exuberance visibly wilted. "But you feel pretty sure?"

Lane faced his horse with his back to Cleeve. He wanted in the worst way to laugh.

Reg answered the question in the same way he'd spoken before. "Maybe. Like I said, wild horses can spook, if a bird flies close, or if they pick up a scent they don't like. Are you goin' to stay here overnight?"

Cleeve had already made arrangements. He would have slept on the ground. Everything he'd been working on for several weeks depended on what happened tomorrow. He said he had hired a room.

Reg made a final remark. "Don't drive your car. Not even here in the town. The noise'll carry. Just settle in. We'll let you know. Do you know where the *cantina* is? Well, go buy yourself a Mexican beer. We'll look you up."

Flor Calderón had remained on the opposite side of the roadway. As Cleeve turned away in the direction of Jacobo's store, she started to cross the road. Out of nowhere, — it seemed to be his habit — Hermangildo Rosas, the *mayordomo,* appeared. They talked near the center of the road. To Lane it didn't look like an argument.

The handsome woman turned back with the Trinity retainer at her side. Once, as they slowly paced toward the upper end of town, Flor Calderón paused to look back. The partners were no longer in sight.

CHAPTER THIRTEEN
MESTEÑOS

Except for Reg's impatience the trap would have worked better. He only wanted to catch the horses. Lane objected on the grounds that man scent was still up there. Reg's answer to that was brusque. "You know how long an animal can live without water? They'll come, an' we got to be close enough to yank the ground cloth." Arguing with Reg Bachelor was like peeing in the ocean with an expectation of raising the tide.

On their way to the trap they saw a pair of riders, loping in the direction of the Trinity yard. Neither of them spoke. Lane was curious. All his partner was interested in was the damned mustangs.

It more than likely wouldn't have worked, if there had been any wind, and this part of Mexico got its share and someone else's share. But not during the still, breathless, hot time of year. Where they hobbled the gray and Lane's bay horse, visibility was excellent. Four-legged critters had scouted up the trap, mostly cattle. They had walked in for water. There were also a few mustang tracks. Several had missed the wings entirely. Those would go thirsty another day or so.

Reg said: "Ten, maybe fifteen head."

They settled where some huge boulders provided seclusion. The rocks offered a variety of shade, but day-long exposure to fierce heat which the rocks absorbed and gave off later made it almost as uncomfortable as being in open country.

As they waited, Lane said: "I'd like to know why Flor went with the foreman."

Reg was mopping sweat and answered without emotion. "When that old son-of-a-bitch says jump in this country, folks ask how high. There's dust!"

Lane saw no dust until he couldn't help but see it. The trap had made the mustangs wary. Everything made wild horses wary, but thirst was a great motivator. The band was heading for the trough as it had done for years. The trap was cause for anxiety, but some of the horses had watered there. They would be spooky, but since nothing had happened before. . . .

Reg built and would have lighted a smoke.

Lane growled. "They'll pick up the scent."

Reg crushed the brown paper cigarette without a word.

Dust was approaching and in this hot country, unlike the high country, it lingered. Eventually it was possible to make out horses, but not individually. They were coming in a bunch, some ahead of the others. Lane had thought a dozen times and continued to think water was the key to catching wild horses, and he was absolutely right, in waterless country anyway. Up north, where they'd wintered, there was water everywhere, but not in this corner of Mexico. There would be a leader. They watched for him, but the fastest animal was a dappled mare with mane and tail flying.

Reg growled. "If that wire don't hold. . . ."

"It held up yonder. Did you hear Jim Lee explain why they used wire instead of solid planks of wood?"

"No."

"Because an eight-hundred-pound horse, hittin' a solid wooden fence, will bust it. The wire gives."

"That dapple mare would make a good race horse."

Lane was sweating. It was hot.

The horses did not slacken their gait until they were almost past the wings, then the uneasiness set in. Several animals hung back, eventually turned, and ran back the way they had come. Reg swore with feeling, pulled his hat forward to shield his eyes, and sat as erectly and stiffly as a ramrod.

The scent of rank sweat carried. Lane got up onto one bent knee, the position of a sprinter. The horses splashed water as they jostled one another. The mare that had led them to the trough put back her ears and lashed out to get room. Opposite her at the trough a rangy stud horse glared. The trough was too wide. He sank his muzzle and noisily drank. The mare did the same.

Lane came up off the ground, running hard. The thirsty animals were fighting to drink. One rawboned, older animal flung up his head and froze. If he had been the mare or the battle-scarred stud horse, he would have whistled, and the band would have charged the opening. Lane's fingers felt like ten thumbs, but he got the wire string and was pulling the ground cloth before terror caused the horses to leave off drinking.

Reg came up. The mustangs could not escape, so they stampeded, hitting each other, tossing their heads. Several whistled but it was too late. They crowded on the far side of the trap, causing the wired sticks to quaver.

Only one horse charged the gate, and, as the two-legged creatures waved their hats and yelled, the horse veered. Ten more feet and he would have broken through the wired ground cloth.

Reg named that horse, the only one that was ever named. "You ory-eyed son-of-a-bitch!"

Lingering dusk helped, but the dust of churned earth did not help visibility. The horses never lost their terror, but they eventually slackened their wild milling a little. One horse swung its head to gulp water, and the other horses knocked it away.

The ground reverberated, dust arose, horses bit one another, pinned their ears back, and lashed out. It was the only thing they thought to do.

Reg yelled: "Sixteen!"

Lane made no attempt to make a count. He was satisfied, however many there were.

An old man from the village came as far as the boulders and stopped. He was expressionless. His name didn't matter, but it was Rafael Yrigoyen. He had been a mustanger during the best years of his life. He remained apart, motionless and expressionless. The partners did not see him. Their position at the gate put their backs to the old man. In fact, they never saw him. He remained for no more than perhaps a half hour, then went trudging back the way he had come. In his ancient way he had bitter thoughts. He and others had wanted the *patrón*'s permission to use the trough as a trap, but, no, the old *pendejo* had allowed *gringos* to use it.

Reg went after a drink of water, by which time the sweat-drenched mustangs had worn themselves down. They still milled on the far side of the trap, as far as they could get from their captors, but since nothing else had happened, they were willing to bunch up, flare out at one another, keep the dust rising.

When Reg returned, he handed Lane two sticks of *charqui*. They were finally able to distinguish one horse from another. Lane was interested in the dappled mare that couldn't be over five or six years of age. Her dapples hadn't begun to fade. Twice she pushed clear to stare at the men. Reg guessed her to be eight hundred pounds, fair size for an inbred wild horse.

The storekeeper with the crooked back drove out with his light dray wagon. He had — of all people — old Dorotea Saenz on the seat with him. He was interested in the captured horses. Dorotea climbed down after only glancing in the direction of the corral, gesturing with both hands at the dust.

She approached Reg from the rear,

tapped his shoulder, handed him a balled-up piece of paper, and returned to the wagon. Jacobo reluctantly turned to drive back to the village. Several times he craned around where the dust was, but old Dorotea did not look back.

Reg pocketed the scrap of paper. Shadows were thickening. He told Lane, if they'd had a few flakes of hay, it would have settled the horses, and got no response for an excellent reason. Lane had seen no put-up hay since he'd been in the area.

Reg finally got to build and light a smoke. He offered the makings, but Lane shook his head. He and the dappled mare were looking steadily at one another. Reg trickled smoke and made another guess. "She's with foal, maybe four, five months."

Several of the horses went back to doing what they'd come to do. They tanked up at the trough. Their boldness set an example. Other horses came to the trough. They were nervous, raised their heads to look at the two-legged things, ducked their heads, and drank. They did not loiter. When they were full, they returned to the band along the far side of the trap.

Horse traps were not only rarely made of solid wood, they were ordinarily made round. Frightened horses — and wild cattle, for that matter — ganged up in corners. Where there were no corners, they were not a danger, either to the confinement or to each other.

Without feed, they had to get word to Cleeve to come for the horses. He had said he'd be in the village, but neither partner had seen him since their last meeting. Someone had to find Cleeve. Lane was willing to make the effort, but he was reluctant. Reg could stand the vigil, but two men at the gate were better than one. Reg had no qualms. He could prevent a break-out. Lane agreed and left the trap to find his horse, remove the hobbles, and head for St. Teresa.

News of their success had preceded them. Jacobo's estimate of the captured mustangs was influenced by his imagination. It wasn't forty head. It wasn't even quite half that number. Since the coming of the *gringos*, several things had changed. One example was the *cantina* proprietor's increased business. Bets had been placed on the number of *mesteños* that had been caught.

Lane found Cleeve among the other patrons of the *cantina*. He had stood several rounds. Not being a beer drinker, Cleeve had matched the salutes of the Mexicans with a jolt of rye whiskey. When Lane found him, Cleeve greeted the younger man with a typical Mexican *abrazo* which not only embarrassed Lane but which almost choked him because of the older man's breath.

Cleeve said he would have the "trookies" at the trap by morning which gratified Lane, but what pleased him more was that the truck had a collapsible ramp for loading.

It was dark, and Lane was hungry. He went to the café of the bearded man, ordered an enchillada and, when it came, the caféman handed over a small bottle of pepper sauce. Lane tried it for one mouthful, drank water, mopped his eyes, and did not touch the small bottle again. Two old men at the counter looked down at their plates. The proprietor, also, showed no expression which wasn't easy to do.

Lane had a tamale wrapped in an ancient newspaper for Reg, and, when he got back, Reg ate the entire tamale without pausing.

The mustangs were becoming as reconciled as they would ever be. While the trough cared for one of their needs, they were tucked up in the flank, and there was nothing that could be done about that. This just was not a country where people cured and stored hay. "How drunk was he?" Reg asked. "If he don't show up tomorrow, I'd say let's turn 'em loose."

Lane had a smoke, then walked slowly around the trap. The horses fidgeted. One animal faced him as he walked. It was the dappled mare. He paused at a place where the crooked fagots permitted him to see inside. The mare pushed her way until she was facing him. She didn't spook. She stood still, looking out at the man who was looking back at her.

Lane talked to the mare, completed his hike, and eased down beside Reg who had done some calculating and had come up with how much Cleeve would owe them. They could have returned to the village, but that would be taking a risk. If something spooked the mustangs badly enough to make them terrified, with no one to deter them they would charge the gate and escape.

Someone was coming on horseback from the direction of the village. The partners waited. With enough moonlight it was eventually possible to see the rider. Lane sighed, and Reg shook his head. He said: "Don't he ever sleep?"

The *mayordomo*, Hermangildo Rosas, rode up, waited to be invited to dismount, and, when Reg grudgingly made the invitation, the older man swung down. He was riding the handsome chestnut that, before his arrival, the partners had only seen Flor Calderón ride.

He came closer, trailing one rein, the other rein looped securely around the saddle horn. He stood briefly silent. It was difficult to read his expression in the poor light.

Reg broke the silence. "Caught a nice band . . . maybe sixteen, eighteen head."

The *mayordomo* glanced briefly where hungry, restless horses were moving. While peering in that direction, he said: "Don Honorio became very sick."

Reg said nothing. Lane did the proper thing. He was sorry. They both were sorry. Was there anything they could do? The *mayordomo* seemed to hesitate before shaking his head. Lane got the impression Rosas had something to say but, upon reflection, had decided not to say it. Instead, he told the partners the old man had been lying on the floor when one of the *vaqueros* had found him. Maybe the old man had been lying there most of the day. Rosas had no idea. He couldn't tell them. They had put him to bed, and the *mayordomo* had ridden to the village to find his granddaughter.

Reg had a question. "How old is he?"

The *mayordomo* was uncertain. In his country few births were recorded, certainly none going back very far. He made a guess. "One hundred?"

Lane remembered the old man had said he was ninety-something.

Reg arose, dusted off, and walked in the direction of the trap. Hermangildo Rosas didn't move. When Reg was far enough away, he said: "The *señorita* wants you to come."

Lane looked up. "Me? She'd want my partner, not me."

"It is the old man. He don't talk good, but she said he wanted to talk to you."

"If he can't talk?"

Rosas shrugged.

Lane faced in the direction of the trap with its noise of troubled animals. "I can't go," he said. "A truck'll be here tomorrow. Me 'n' Reg got to be here to help load."

There was the matter of being paid. All they knew about Cleeve was that he spent much of his time over the line in San Diego. It wasn't that they didn't trust him, not entirely anyway; it was that they didn't know him well enough.

The *mayordomo* repeated himself and added to it that the old man was very ill. It was the duty of the healthy to obey the wishes of the very ill. In a lowered voice Rosas said: "He will die of a certainty. Tomorrow . . . maybe not then . . . but surely the day after."

Reg returned, reacted to the thick silence by looking from Lane to the Mexican and back. As he sat down, he said: "Something's wrong. The truck isn't coming?"

Lane explained. Reg reacted predictably. He had no use for Don Honorio. He told Hermangildo Rosas neither partner could leave, but that, as soon as the horses were loaded and gone, both he and Lane would ride over.

The *mayordomo* made one of those fluttery gestures with both arms, mounted the handsome chestnut, and reined away without another word, or the customary salute.

Reg watched the Mexican until he was lost in the poor visibility, then he spoke while still squinting in the direction of faint horse sounds. "The old son-of-a-bitch isn't any one hundred years old. But he's old for a fact, an' from his foreman's face I'd guess they expect the old bastard to die."

Lane had a sudden and unprecedented change of thought. "He's got one hell of a ranch. Owns land in all directions . . . farther than you can see."

"Yeah, an' his measly Trinity cows. He should have weeded out and brought in upgrade replacements. Lane, they do everything in this country the way their granddaddies did."

Lane took a different tack. "Suppose a man owned one of these old grants, thousands of acres, more cattle than a man could count?"

Reg snorted and rose to dust off. "He'd never sell. Fellers like Don Honorio would die before selling off land. He didn't even want the runty mustangs disturbed. Fellers like him stop advancing . . . spend their lives in a rut." Reg rolled and lighted a smoke, offered the makings.

While Lane was creating his own cigarette, he privately decided not to carry this conversation to its conclusion. He had heard his partner's snort of derision.

All the mustangs never completely settled down, but some of them did. Reg and Lane took turns, remaining awake. When first light appeared, Lane went back to the village to find Cleeve and the truck.

While he was gone, the dappled mare nickered. Reg went over to find her. Something was bothering her. She didn't seem concerned with his presence. She paced, sipped water, menaced other animals with flattened ears, and Reg decided she had to be horsing. He was unmindful that was not possible; she was carrying a colt.

He heard the truck at about the same time he saw its dust. A few yards ahead was Cleeve's unwashed Dodge car. Off to one side and loping was Lane. Reg watched, swore to himself. The let-down tailgate of the truck was half the width of the gate. It would take some fancy foot work to prevent terrified wild horses from going around both sides of the ramp.

Cleeve batted at dust with his hat while he arm-signaled to the truck driver as he backed the truck close to the gate. The driver did a fair job. At least, when his ramp was lowered, no horses could get around it on the driver's side. On the opposite side the gap was a good six or eight feet.

Reg left it to his partner, Cleeve, and the trucker to let down the loading ramp. He went to the opposite side, waved with his hat so the horses would crowd toward the ramp.

The driver was a short, stocky man who looked to be either a *gachupín* or half Anglo. He was business-like. He had backed up the way he had, deliberately to preclude escape on his side. Allowing a gap on both sides would almost guarantee that some of the wildly agitated mustangs would charge blindly. His way they could only successfully do that on the far side. Lane left Cleeve and the trucker, went over to support Reg, and, when Cleeve flung the ground cloth aside and dropped its supporting wire, two mustangs charged, hit the ramp, and went up into the truck. Dust arose; men whooped; horses followed the first two.

One animal hung back, veered to the far side and made a dash. Reg jumped to block the opening, waving his hat. Lane came close, bumped his partner hard enough for Reg to drop the hat as he staggered to regain his balance. The dappled mare flew past, reached the end of the wings, and kept on running.

Reg picked up his hat, glared, and moved closer to prevent any more escapes.

CHAPTER FOURTEEN
A SHOCKER

They never saw the dappled mare again, but after the truck and Cleeve left, Reg entered the empty trap, splashed water in his face, and turned. "That wasn't no accident. You knocked me off balance so's that mare could get away."

Lane was vigorously scratching. Thick dust always had that effect on him. "You brought along the ridgling. The mare didn't want to go to the killer, an' I didn't want her to."

Reg growled. "Cost us money." He went to work making a smoke. Lane stripped to the waist at the stone trough to wash himself off in the sun, when his partner said: *"Son-of-a-bitch!"* He was holding the scrap of paper he'd gotten from Dorotea Saenz which he'd forgotten until this moment.

Lane was putting on his shirt again. "What is it?"

Reg handed over the crumpled slip of paper. Lane read it twice, looked over at his partner. "I've been in this country before, but damned if I'll ever understand these

215

people. How did the old woman know?"

Reg didn't answer. He was staring into the distance.

Lane handed back the piece of paper. "I don't much care for their *cerveza*, but let's go back to town."

The *cantina* was nearly empty. The rotund proprietor smiled broadly and congratulated them in Spanish which neither of them understood but smiled back anyway and asked for *dos cervezas*.

Wizened old Rafael Yrigoyen said something to the proprietor who quickly produced two large glasses of tepid beer.

Lane turned and thanked the wizened old man. He hadn't seen him at the trap the day or so before. What intrigued him was that he would have bet his life the old man hadn't spoken in Spanish.

He was right. Rafael Yrigoyen had spoken in Basque. The proprietor was also Basque. In Mexico there were Basques. They passed easily as Mexicans; the very fair ones passed for *gachupins*. Not that any of it mattered.

The beer tasted neither good nor bad. Afterward, they returned to the fresh air and heat. Several children with their invariable long-tailed, thin dogs were playing in the mud near the bricked up well.

The old Basque followed them outside

and spoke English. "It's strange that Don Calderón would let two *gringos* trap horses. It's never happened before." Rafael Yrigoyen smiled and walked away. They would never see him again. In fact, not until years later when they encountered a *gringo* named Yrigoyen near the California town of Calabasas would they know what a Basque was.

They went to wash the backs of their horses out behind the Saenz house. Doing anything that required water was a pleasure. Full summer was on in arid Mexico. There were few people abroad. A centuries-old custom kept them indoors behind mud walls three feet thick during the day.

It was the time of *siesta*. Supper would be between nine and ten o'clock, after the sun and most of the heat were gone. But not everyone slept. Old Dorotea came out where the horses were being sluiced. She ignored Lane, looking steadily at Reg. "Well, *gringo?*"

Reg used his shirt tail to dry hands and face. He was tucking it in, when he looked steadily at the old woman. "That's crazy."

Dorotea shrugged bony shoulders. "How else?" she asked.

"Not like that for chris' sake."

Lane hadn't been able to understand

more than a couple of words. The note had been too ragged and scrawled.

Dorotea shrugged again. "She is not young. Also, at her advanced age women do crazy things, if they think they are losing maybe their only chance. You can understand that?"

Reg's expression showed clearly that he did not understand. Dorotea contemptuously said — *"Gringos!"* — and stamped back into the coolness of her house.

Lane had a question. "What was that about?"

"You read the gawd-damned note!"

Lane went after the old woman, catching her at the door. "What does *muerta* mean?"

Her gaze was like ice. "Death. It means what the note said. Flor could take no more. She told me this would be her last chance."

"She killed herself?" Lane asked incredulously.

"No, *estúpido!* She killed the old man!"

Lane stared without speaking. "Her grandfather for chris' sake?"

Dorotea hung fire before speaking again. "Come inside."

Lane followed. The old woman dug out a dusty bottle of red wine, half filled two glasses, set one glass before Lane, sat opposite him on a handmade bench, drank half her glass empty, and fixed him with a fierce look. "It is true. You *do* look like him!"

"What the hell are you talking about?"

Dorotea Saenz finished her wine, put the glass down hard, and made a death's head smile. "Why did he let you trap horses? He's never permitted anyone else even to think of such a thing. Did he talk much to you?"

"Well, we visited, if that's what you mean."

"You see, *gringo*. You look enough like his son to be him, except for the light hair. Even the eyes . . . steely blue. I don't know where he got such color eyes." Dorotea refilled her glass before continuing. "Flor said it to me. *Gringos* call it reincarnation. Someone returns from the dead. You were to him the son who died years ago."

"He showed me an old photograph. . . ."

Dorotea smiled bitterly. "I gave him that picture . . . Don Honorio was his father. I was his mother. Why do you think I let you use my corral? Get the bottle, refill your glass."

The old woman blew her nose lustily in an ancient handkerchief. Lane understood something that had mystified him. The reason the old woman refused to go out to the Calderón place. While he was refilling his glass, he said: "Did Flor know?"

"She knew. She, too, saw the likeness. She said it troubled her grandfather very much. She said it was that thing."

"Reincarnation?"

"Yes. It was the reincarnation. It frightened her. She told me Don Honorio couldn't sleep. She said he prayed almost all one night. His gratitude to God for sending his son back."

Without touching his refilled glass, Lane wagged his head. As his partner had said, they had come down here to trap wild horses, a simple, if arduous and difficult, way to make money. For chris' sake. That's all they'd come to do.

Dorotea said: "It killed his *señora*. She would hardly come to the village. People might know, and they would laugh behind her back. They didn't know. How could they? Only he and I knew. My husband was alive then." Dorotea wiped her eyes and blew her nose again, took down a ragged big breath, and looked at Lane. "Flor was a beautiful girl. He shouldn't have sent her to the *yanquis* to be educated. You don't understand? She is old by our standard. This would be her last chance. She told me that, and cried. Your friend is as thick as oak."

"She didn't have to kill him, Dorotea. She could have gone somewhere."

"Would your friend go with her?"

Lane avoided an answer, pushed the wine aside. "I've got to go outside."

"And tell your friend?"

Lane hesitated in the doorway. "No. Someday, maybe."

The heat hit him hard. Reg was skiving water off his gray horse which seemed to enjoy being wet all over. His old wound left a slight, sunken place, but the hair had grown back.

As Lane approached, someone hailed them from alongside the house. It was Cleeve, sweaty, dusty, but smiling. He had been with the truck, when it crossed out of Mexico and was stopped on the other side.

Cleeve shook his head. "Branding them was like a war. I'll get your money by the time you catch another band. Lane, you look worried."

Reg glanced at his partner. "Not another scorpion I hope."

Cleeve wanted to get out of the heat. It was a long drive to San Diego. He wanted to be there when the mustangs were unloaded. He couldn't possibly make it.

After he left, they tied the horses in some shade and went around to the *cantina* where the Mexican-looking Basque proprietor grinned and set up two bottles of beer. His place was empty except for a thin dog, sleeping in a corner. Conversation was out of the question, although the proprietor tried, gave up, shrugged, and set up another pair of bottled beers.

Lane felt the second one. He sweated and slumped. Reg said they'd ought to go see if they could find another band and drift them closer. Lane shook his head. He wanted to sleep somewhere in shade. Reg was agreeable. The place where they found a modicum of shade was in a crooked alleyway behind that low-walled corral where the big *yanqui* mule came over in its expressionless way and watched them settle.

Somewhere not too distant a dog fight erupted. It was accompanied by much yelling and cursing in Spanish until one dog yelped, when he'd been kicked, and the fight and noise ended.

Lane lay back with his hat tipped, and peeked from beneath the black brim at a pale and cloudless sky. For a fact, the old man had seemed to have taken to him, more noticeably than he'd taken to Reg. Lane closed his eyes. At least up north the Mormons had pretty much left them alone. There had been no familial entanglements. They'd been hired to trap horses; otherwise, they'd been left alone. In Mexico it seemed a man couldn't even pee without some kind of social involvement.

He had been in Mexico before. In fact, he'd come close to getting married and might have except that he'd never kissed the lovely young *señorita*. The reason was simple. She had a downy, black mustache. He had never been able to figure a tactful way of mentioning a razor. On such delicate matters romances perished.

Killed the old son-of-a-bitch! Over something Lane was fairly sure Reg did not even suspect! He nudged his partner. "One more load," he said, "and let's get the hell out of this country."

Reg didn't reply. He was sleeping like the dead.

Alfredo, the *vaquero* who had found Don Honorio, appeared in St. Teresa, ostensibly to get the mail, actually to find the *gringos*. He was told at the *cantina* they had been seen sitting in shade on the bench out front of the store. Alfredo went over there only to be told the *gringos* had left earlier, had ridden in the direction of the trap to which Jacobo added that only *norteamericanos* and the red flaggers, the rural police known as *rurales,* rode out during the hot time of the day.

The *siesta* in the alley had helped as had a

meal at the long, narrow cookery of the man with the splendid beard, but Lane was unusually quiet. So quiet in fact that Reg looked over, scowling. "You feel all right?"

"I'd feel better, if we were back over the border."

"Is something wrong?"

Lane looked squarely at his partner. "Wrong? What could be wrong in a place where it's hotter'n hell?"

They did not push the horses, and, although they rode until sundown, they saw neither mustangs nor their dust. Reg argued with himself. "It's the only water for a hundred miles, for chris' sake. They got to be out there. Maybe we should go talk to the *mayordomo*. If anyone would know, he would."

To Lane that was not a good idea. "We'll head out before sunup tomorrow. If they're out there, we'll find 'em."

Reg was agreeable but unconvinced. "Cleeve'll be showin' up, screamin' like a wounded eagle for more horses."

Lane repeated something. "The sooner I'm out of this country the better I'll like it."

For all his partner's shortcomings, after years of association Reg knew Lane as well as Lane knew him. "What's botherin' you?"

"Mexicans."

Reg shrugged. "When you're in Rome, you wear a toga. . . ."

Lane looked around. "Flor Calderón's quite a woman."

His partner agreed in a way that made Lane roll his eyes. Reg said: "You could do a heap worse. That old bastard won't live forever. You'd own the whole shebang."

The trap had been used not only by cattle. There were also the smallish, unshod hoof sign of mustangs. Reg was smug. "For a damned fact, this's got to be the only water hole for one hell of a distance. You ready?"

They turned back. The trap hadn't been seriously damaged. A few fagots had been cracked, but the circle was as sound as new money.

Lane took his partner to the *cantina* and encountered something different from the ordinarily good-natured greetings. They were looked upon by expressionless dark men, some smoking, some with *cerveza* before them. The Basque set up full glasses without speaking. An old man said something, and the proprietor shot him a venomous look.

Outside, Reg said: "Kind of cool in there."

Lane nodded. They needed a place to bed

down. When that had been satisfactorily attended to, Lane had another night of spotty sleep.

Killed the old bastard? His own granddaughter for chris' sake!

In the morning they had breakfast and headed for the trap. It had been visited, mostly by horses this time. Reg smiled. "Easy as falling off a log. If every set-up was like this one, I'd say let's stay in the business an' let the water holes do it for us."

They decided that, although the latest band of horses was not large, they would trap them anyway. Lane thought of a dozen reasons for this, and Reg was agreeable. He would have preferred waiting for a large band, but something was bothering his partner.

Back in the village that coolness was noticeable. It baffled Reg that his partner wanted so badly to end this Mexican, wild-horse business, but he would go along. It was a big world, and there were other places.

Dorotea Saenz met them leaving the eatery. To Lane it seemed to be something close to entrapment. She didn't smile, and her words were brusque. "There is a *gringo* in a car looking for you."

Reg nodded. "Cleeve. Let's go back to the saloon."

Dorotea's attitude did not change. "No! Flor Calderón is at my house. She wants to see . . . this one." There was no mistaking the pointed finger.

Lane was groping, when his partner did it for him. He told the old woman they'd come around, after they'd tended their horses.

Lane scotched their usual place for washing horses' backs by leading his horse in the direction of the place with the too-low adobe corral where its inhabitant lived — the big *yanqui* mule with the solemn, almost sad expression. They off-rigged, found a pair of dented tin buckets that leaked, and went to work.

Reg was hungry. There were times when Lane had considered giving his partner a worm pill. He could eat any time night or day, a sure sign of worms.

It was impossible to wash horses with leaking buckets and not get well soaked. The heat, even at sundown and later, was a blessing. They went to the elongated, narrow restaurant and got fed by an un-smiling woman of respectable proportions who they assumed was the caféman's wife.

While they were there, Jacobo, the storekeeper, came in, walked close, and whispered. *"El patrón is dead."*

Reg was pushing his plate away and commented without looking away from what he was doing. *"Bueno, el bastardo viejo."*

The sturdy woman looked shocked. Jacobo said: "You're learning. But I wouldn't say it too much. He was not liked, but of the dead. . . ." He crossed himself, and left. The caféman's woman stood like stone, looking straight at Reg.

Lane paid and led the way outside. If there was a lighted candle at Dorotea's house, it was not visible. Reg was sucking his teeth. "You want to go over there?"

"No. Where the hell is Cleeve?"

"You don't like the old woman? She means well. She's harmless."

Lane dryly agreed. "Yeah, real harmless."

Lane was saved from having to protest further. Cleeve appeared down near the general store and let go with a yell that would have wakened the dead. When he caught up with them, he fished in a pocket, brought forth a soiled fold of *yanqui* greenbacks, peeled off two separate sets, and handed one to Reg, and one to Lane.

Reg was impressed. "Your folks up yonder pay well."

Cleeve ignored that. "They need that

many more. Twice that many, if you can trap them."

Cleeve had been drinking, not enough to do damage, but to Lane he always seemed different when he'd been drinking. He was more open and affable. Lane told Cleeve they would work the trap tomorrow, and Cleeve showed such pleasure that, as he was walking away, Reg said: "There's times when he's almost human."

"Yeah. When he's been to the saloon."

Across the wide, dusty roadway they had their second encounter. The *mayordomo* was over there, mostly hidden by the blighted light of evening. They didn't see him until they were almost to the far side, then he spoke cordially in Spanish. Lane nodded. The *mayordomo* was not smiling. He usually smiled, when they met. He said: "The *señorita* is at the old woman's *choza*."

Lane nodded.

Hermangildo Rosas had more to say. "Don Honorio died of the mal seizure." Rosas softly raised and dropped his shoulder. "It was time. Not many live to his age."

Reg was eyeing the older man closely. "Does that mean we can't trap any more horses?"

"No. Not if you were permitted."

Reg relaxed. As far as he was concerned, no further discussion was necessary.

Lane had questions which the *mayordomo* answered with what appeared to be truthful frankness. He had never been an easy man for Lane to understand.

"There will be another truck tomorrow or the next day . . . after we trap more horses," Lane explained.

Rosas nodded, occasionally switching his attention to Reg. When Lane was satisfied all that needed to be said had been said, he was willing to part company.

The *mayordomo* said — "The *señorita* is waiting." — and expected a different answer than the one he got.

Reg was obviously no longer interested, since the question of additional trapping had been settled. He said: "We have some work to do on the trap."

Rosas's eyebrows climbed. "The *señorita?*"

Reg shrugged. "*Seguro,* we'll go see her."

The *mayordomo* finally smiled slightly, but it was still a smile.

Lane watched the older man walk away. He pondered telling Reg what old Dorotea had said, and also shrugged as Reg started in the direction of the Saenz house.

CHAPTER FIFTEEN
ANOTHER CRISIS

The handsome chestnut horse was dozing in the shade. Lane hung back. Inside, there was a furious argument in progress. Lane could pick up only an occasional word. Reg looked around, obviously of the opinion that this might not be a good time to visit. He turned back the way they had come. The angry voices were audible as far as the roadway. Reg shook his head. He had several times intruded in arguments between women, and each time the women had turned on him with venom. As they walked away, he said: "Another time, maybe."

It was a little early for bedding down in the alley, but they went up there anyway. As they were exchanging stares with the big, gaunt mule, Reg said: "I got a feeling something's going on . . . you?"

Lane nodded, as he eased down with his back to the mule's low, mud wall. "The old man's dead."

"But the foreman said we could still use the trap."

Lane looked at his partner. "That note

from Flor Calderón. She wanted to see us . . . mainly you."

Reg squirmed to get comfortable. The mule leaned over and nudged Reg's hat, knocking it off. Reg knocked off alleyway dust and reset the hat, calling the mule a bad name.

Lane said: "She killed the old man."

"What? Who killed the old man?"

"Flor Calderón."

"What in hell are you talking about!"

"The old woman told me, while you were out with the horses."

Reg saw the moving shadow, ducked, and swung an open hand. It caught the mule on the nose. The mule ducked back and walked to another part of the goat pen or whatever the low, mud wall had been used for. "She didn't . . . Dorotea is old. She made that up. Why would . . . ?"

"You noticed how the villagers looked at us? Somehow they knew."

Reg fumbled for his makings and went to work, scowling and building a cigarette. "How would the old woman know? It don't make sense."

Lane could have agreed with that. "The note . . . she wanted to see you."

"Well, what's that got to do with Dorotea's crazy idea?"

"Dorotea told me, when women get along toward Flor's age, they get sort of desperate. Reg, she wants you real bad. The old woman said Flor figures it's her last chance to get a man."

Reg deeply inhaled, exhaled, and gazed at his partner. "I don't believe any of this, an', besides, I've never touched her, so why should she think . . . ? This is what's been bothering you?"

"Yes."

Reg stubbed out his smoke. "It's not true, but, if it was, no man in his right mind would court a woman who kills people. I'd like to find the *mayordomo*."

"You know why the old man let us trap horses? He's never allowed it before. He and old Dorotea had a son. I look like him. The old man . . . this sounds crazier by the minute . . . the old man believed I was his son come back to life."

"So we could trap horses?"

"Something like that. Old Dorotea. . . ."

"Lane, you know what? She's crazier'n a pet 'coon. You believe any of this?"

Lane was slow answering, and, when he did answer, it wasn't a direct response. "I just want to get the hell out of here. One more band, an' they can have this country."

Reg went to work rolling another smoke.

He offered the sack to Lane, who shook his head. After lighting up, Reg quietly said: "I'll be gawd-damned. Come to think about it, she was real friendly. I still say Dorotea is full of bull. She made that up sure as we're sittin' here."

Lane looked dispassionately at his partner. "You're thicker'n stone."

Reg did as he'd done before. He stubbed out his half-smoked cigarette, relaxed against the low wall at his back, and sank into an impenetrable silence.

Dusk came. Lane was getting hungry. He arose, dusted off, and said: "I can stand about one more Mex supper. You coming?"

Reg looked up. "Do you believe all this crap . . . that she killed the old man?"

"I know how to find out."

"Go out yonder and look up the *mayordomo?*"

"No. Go talk to Dorotea. Maybe Flor will be there, but I wouldn't be. Not after a shoutin' match like they had."

"Let's go. Do you believe in reincarnation?"

Lane answered. "I can't even spell it." He reset his hat. For about the tenth time he thought all they'd come here for was to trap wild horses, and for a fact it was the best set-up for trapping them, the only water for miles. As they started walking, in the direction of the old woman's house, he also wished they'd never met Henry Cleeve.

Dorotea's house showed feeble candlelight through its only window. It faced the roadway. The chestnut horse was gone. Lane knocked on the door three times. There was no response.

Reg said: "Try the door."

It opened on silent, leather hinges. The candle was two-thirds burned down on its plate. It cast no more light inside than outside. The place had a peculiar odor. Other times, when Lane had been inside, the smell was of cooking. He couldn't place the present aroma. It wasn't sweet. Its faint sourness was not especially objectionable.

The old woman was hunched over at the table, her back to them. She didn't move. The upset bottle of wine was responsible for the smell. She had put both arms atop the table with her head down upon them.

Reg walked close, looked up, and said: "Drunker'n a skunk."

From within the folded arms Dorotea said — "She was going to hit me." — and made no effort to raise her head. "It was the truth, and she knew it. She said it has always been a secret. I told her, no, people see things. Him visiting, staying the night, me getting bigger by the month." It required an effort, but the old woman raised her head. Her face was swollen, and tears still trickled. "I said she shouldn't have hurt him. He was old. He would go soon."

Reg kicked a small bench around, sat on it, and looked at his partner. He had never been able to handle tears very well, particularly female tears.

Lane went to the bench he'd used previously which was opposite Dorotea. "Did she say why she killed her grand-father?"

"She became very angry. She said he was almost dead when she got there. Hermangildo and the *vaqueros* had cared for him. She said he couldn't talk, but in his eyes she saw the fury at her. She said . . . he died straining to speak . . . he tried to sit up. She said he would have cursed her . . . he sat up, got very red in the face, and fell back dead." Dorotea considered the spilled red wine and its bottle on the floor near her left foot. "She said it was my fault. All I'd have had to do was not let him into the house. She said, if my husband hadn't been out with the sheep and goats, he would have killed Don Honorio. What she said was right. I shouldn't have let him inside, but he was *el patrón*. You don't close doors in the face of the *patrón*."

Dorotea looked down again at the bottle. It wasn't quite empty. When she leaned to retrieve it, if Reg hadn't moved fast, she would have fallen. He settled her back on the bench, got the bottle, and placed it in front of her. He looked over her head. His partner ignored him.

Lane had a question. "But you told me earlier she had killed him. Why?"

"She did. He wouldn't have taken the seizure, but for her telling him she would go away with . . . him." Dorotea glared straight at Reg. "He was a proud man. From a long line of proud *gachupíns*."

Lane rolled his eyes. *These gawd-damned people . . . a man finds a perfect place for trapping wild horses . . . maybe not another place like it for a thousand miles. What should have been straightforwardly simple got so complicated. . . .* He went to the rear door and stood looking out at the corral. He heard Reg scrape the floor with the bench as he arose and didn't face around.

Dorotea wasn't finished. "You," she said to Reg. "Why didn't you stay in your own country? Why you? She has had many men to visit. Her grandfather ran them off. Not good enough for a Calderón. And you came, a *gringo*. The old man hated *gringos*. His father hated them. She was no longer young. Soon to be too old for children. You came and she . . . I know her temper. I know what she called the old man, and he fell to the floor . . . couldn't talk. That's what killed him. Her own grandfather, may God forgive her. And you . . . !"

Reg picked up the nearly empty wine bottle, set it squarely in front of the old woman, put it down hard. "Drink it," he snarled, jerked his head, and both *gringos* left the house.

It was hot. The village seemed deserted. A long-tailed, gaunt dog was sniffing at the roadside. Out of nowhere a larger dog appeared and charged the gaunt dog. It tucked its tail and fled.

Lane said: "Catch as many as we can tomorrow an' get the hell out of here."

Reg was not in a mood to agree or disagree. He said nothing until a horseman loped into sight from the north, an accomplished rider whose britches never left the leather. Lane groaned to himself. *Mayordomo* Rosas!

They waited in front of Jacobo Figuero's store. The centaur saw them and reined toward a tie pole nearby, looped his reins, and walked toward them, his Chihuahua spur rowels making tiny puffs of dust rise. He wasn't smiling.

Reg's mood was reflected in his face as he met the older man.

Rosas said: "Where is she?"

Lane softly scowled. "Who?"

"The *señorita*. She's here, I think. Where else? When I told you she was waiting to see you, she was here. She came to the house, then left again. I sent for the *padre*. We have the grave ready. We are to bury her grandfather at dawn. Where is she?"

Lane answered honestly. "I got no idea. We haven't seen her."

The *mayordomo* stood like a dark, weathered statue, looking from one of them to the other. Eventually he said: "She left on the chestnut horse. The riders saw her. She was coming in this direction." He briefly brightened. "To the Saenz house," he said, and turned to recross the roadway.

Lane called after him. "We just came from there. She isn't there."

Rosas turned in the center of the roadway for a moment, then continued walking in the direction of the Saenz house.

Reg was watching the *mayordomo*. "Leave 'em be. They're as crazy as a bunch of coots. Let's go out to the trap and get ready for morning."

They went much farther. They read sign and studied distances for dust. It was on their way back with evening approaching that they saw dust, and, as they sat still, they also saw the cause of the dust. A band of horses was coming — not from the west but from the north. Lane led off for those huge, old rocks southwest of the trap.

It would be dusk, maybe later, before the wild horses reached the trough inside the trap. Impaired visibility would favor the mustangers and most likely a powerful thirst. Reg's mood changed. For the time being anyway, nothing mattered but what was shortly to take place. Lane was the silent, troubled one. The chase and its likely successful conclusion were foremost, but other things were indelibly imprinted, and they would remain so for many years.

The horses were moving fast. Lane had no idea how far the scent of water carried, but it had to be quite a distance. Some Trinity cattle put their tails up like scorpions and scattered in every direction as the running horses came unerringly forward.

Reg hobbled the gray horse. Lane followed that example. Huge rocks served a purpose, but they weren't worth a damn to tie horses to.

Reg let out a squawk and threw up his right arm. There was a distant rider, scarcely visible, far behind the mustangs and slightly westerly. "If they see him back there," Reg exclaimed, "they'll scatter to hell and back! What's that son-of-a-bitch doin' out there, anyway?"

Lane remained silent. It was true. If just two or three mustangs looked in the direction of the distant rider, the entire band would split in a dozen directions. Not only that, but they would not return possibly for days, possibly never. Thirst was a powerful motivator, but fear of losing life was even greater, and wild horses lived daily with that fear.

Reg reset his hat to block late-day sunlight. Neither he nor Lane moved nor scarcely breathed. Eventually the mustangs would see that rider. When they stormed into the trap for water, they would be as wary as most wild things were.

Lane tried to watch the horseman through a high banner of dust as the horses got closer. If the rider knew the wild horses were a mile or more ahead — and he should know because of the dust — he was neither changing his course nor boosting over into a gait faster than a slow lope.

Reg's jaw muscles were quivering. Otherwise, he was as still as a statue. Eventually he spoke without looking around at Lane. "If they scatter, we might as well go home.

That son-of-a-bitch!"

Lane was totally still. He didn't pray. He wasn't a praying man, but if he had been, he would have prayed hard. The alternative was one long moment of mental torture. As Reg had said, if they lost this band, they might as well forget mustanging. Actually Lane was not convinced he wanted to follow the dog-food route anyway. That dead mare and colt he'd seen back on the reservation had scarred him for life. He would never forget that as long as he lived.

Reg made an explosive curse. The distant rider had boosted his mount over into one of those long-legged lopes that amounted to a run. The mustangs were dark with sweat. They surely had the scent by now. They were roughly a half mile away, sun-glow reflected off their sweaty hides. It became possible to make out individual animals. The one that held Lane's attention was a stocky bay stallion with a thick mane and tail. He was in the lead. There were finer built, taller horses, but they seemed unwilling to challenge the bay stallion by racing past him.

Reg made a rough guess. "Twenty-five."

Lane hoped not that many. Twenty-five wild horses, hitting their trap together, would demolish it. Lane said: "Morgan.

Where in hell did a Morgan horse come from in this country?" He was wrong. The hairy, stocky stallion wasn't a Morgan horse, but he had been endowed with all the right characteristics, which, while unusual among mustangs, were not entirely unique.

Dust scent carried as far as the mammoth rocks. Without any reason that the watchers could see, an older, flat-chinned, gaunt horse jammed around in a sliding halt, flung up its head, and swerved violently about a hundred yards from the wings of the trap. Lane swore. The old mustang had seen the oncoming rider.

As the other horses stormed around him, bumping and pushing, to reach the trough, the old horse trumpeted, a sound barely audible over the sounds of horses lunging toward water, squealing, pinning back their ears, snapping with bared teeth to reach the trough. There was no mistaking the stance of the old horse. Thirsty or not, the greater fear made him whistle again. He might as well not have made a sound. But as the other horses ran past, the old horse swung fully to face the far-away rider and race back past the wings to freedom.

Lane and Reg didn't move until the old horse was well clear of the wings. If other horses had heeded his warning, they could not have reached the ground-cloth gate in time, but only the old horse ran belly down in the opposite direction.

Lane passed Reg in a furious race to reach the gate. Reg was close, but Lane yanked up the wire and was tugging the ground cloth when his partner reached him. Some of the horses flung up their dripping muzzles. The others did not react until at least most of their thirst was taken care of.

Reg was trying to make a gate count. Three times he broke off to swear and start over.

Lane was beginning to itch. The dust was thick and cloud-like. The distant rider dropped down to a long-legged walk and was heading straight for the trap. Reg said: "Run the son-of-a-bitch off. We got our hands full."

Lane ignored the admonition. An occasional mustang would feint in the direction of the gate, but mostly they crowded against the far fence, and despite their noise — and the dust — Reg and Lane could hear the fagots creak as the wire yielded when horses pushed hard.

CHAPTER SIXTEEN
THE UNEXPECTED

If they'd had hay as they'd had up yonder, it most likely wouldn't have made any difference. These mustangs would have trampled it. The partners waved with their hats and shouted, when horses came toward the ground-cloth gate. It worked possibly more from scent than from the gesticulations.

Dust reached fetlock height and would rise higher. Reg was trying to count again. Lane stopped flagging with his hat and was standing still. That solitary rider was approaching in an easy slow lope. There was dust but not enough to obscure the horseman.

Lane spoke to himself. "*Her!* For chris' sake . . . Reg." He had to call louder. Reg turned, looked past, and became motionless.

Flor Calderón rode as far as the big rocks, swung off, knelt to use rawhide hobbles on the handsome chestnut horse, rose, dusted off and walked in the direction of the trap. When she was close enough, she ignored Lane to address his partner.

"Are you satisfied?"

Reg scowled. "Satisfied . . . ?"

"When it was allowed, when my father was alive, it was the custom to catch them with water." She jutted her jaw toward the chestnut horse. On both sides of her *silla de vaquero* were flattened, waterproof canvas buckets. "Find them, then trickle water." She faced Reg. "They scent the water and follow it."

Reg removed his hat, scratched, and dropped the hat back on. "Say that again . . . you went 'way out there with buckets of water and trickled it so's they would follow?"

She smiled for the first time, and Lane, who hadn't said a word, told himself again that she was a handsome woman.

Reg said: "I'll be damned."

She laughed, showing perfect white teeth and one dimple. She came closer. The mustangs were still agitated. She nodded toward Lane and raised her voice. "I rode for hours." Her dark eyes twinkled. "Do I get a share?"

Lane smiled back. "Take your pick."

She didn't hesitate. "The brown stallion with the thick mane and tail."

Reg dryly said: "He's a fightin' son-of-a-bitch."

She turned her smile to Reg. "A good stud fights for what he wants."

Lane was shocked. The way she was regarding his partner left no doubt about her meaning. If Reg caught the innuendo, he showed no sign of it when he spoke. "Rosas was looking for you in the village. He sent somewhere for a priest. They have the grave dug."

Her smile wilted. She slowly turned toward Lane. He shrugged. She went to the ground cloth to consider the horses. Without looking around she said: "Twenty-three."

Both men accepted her count. Reg went up beside her. Lane was beginning to itch. The dust was less now than it had been, but it was still uncomfortably airborne. The mustangs did not slacken off in their terror. The horses they had trapped up north had eventually settled. These horses did not.

Flor Calderón turned toward Reg. "You will send for the truck?"

He nodded, watching the horses, not her. "In the morning." He finally faced her. "You're a long way from home, an' it'll be dark directly."

She offered a delayed reply. "I don't want to go back there."

Reg acted nonplused. "It's your home, Flor."

She returned to watching the mustangs. "Will you tell me the truth, if I ask you a question?"

Reg could see Lane scratching to one side and showed how much he had learned south of the border by shrugging.

She laughed at him before speaking. "Dorotea Saenz told me neither of you is married."

Reg nodded. "Someday maybe, but not for a while yet."

"Why? You don't like women?"

"I like 'em," Reg replied, looking in at the horses. "I've never known very many. My mother, one named. . . ."

"Elaine," Lane said.

His partner nodded. "Elaine. Red-headed with freckles."

Lane said: "Tell her the rest of it."

Reg squinted. "We were going to get married. Lane came by to say he was heading north."

Lane went on. "He threw his outfit in with mine, and we started for Colorado. On the trail we met Elaine and her father on the way to the church. I waved. Reg sunk down, and maybe she's still waiting at the church with her dad."

Flor Calderón turned large, dark eyes on Reg. "At the church. You were supposed to be married?"

"Yes'm."

She turned to studying the horses. Dust was settling. Her chestnut horse nickered. It was either thirsty or hungry, or maybe both. Flor Calderón turned toward Lane. "Go with me to my horse," she said and led the way, leaving Reg to mind the gate. As she stooped to remove the braided, rawhide hobbles, she said: "Did he really do that?"

Lane answered succinctly and truthfully. "Yes'm. When we got back in autumn, she was waiting."

Flor straightened up to drape the hobbles behind the cantle and abruptly turned. "He had a reason?"

"It was time to head for the high country. We did it every spring . . . worked the ranches and headed back come fall."

"And she was waiting? I'd have killed him."

Lane stopped scratching. "He didn't want . . . it was her idea . . . she pushed real hard."

"Then he didn't love her?"

"I'd guess not. We were gone almost until the first frost. It was a good year. We got paid regularly, liked the work, and. . . ."

"Is he capable of love?"

Lane scratched. "Everyone's capable of love, ma'am."

She mounted in one smooth movement, evened up her reins, and barely nodded as she rode away. Lane could hear the horse long after he lost sight of it.

Reg was smoking, when Lane went back to the gate. Reg put a quizzical look on his partner, and Lane said: "She asked questions about you. Reg, old Dorotea's right. *Gringo* or not, Flor Calderón's taken a shine to you."

Reg blew smoke, watched the horses begin to settle a little. "When's Cleeve due back?"

"Maybe tomorrow. He can't haul all those horses. That truck he used last time isn't big enough. You want to let her have the Morgan-built horse?"

"You?"

"If she wants it. We owe her that 'n' more. Next time we'll know how to bait 'em with water."

Reg reacted waspishly. "Not here. Not anywhere even near here. You really want to go into this mustangin' business?"

"Not in Mexico, an' maybe nowhere else, if all they're going to do is make dog food out of 'em. Reg . . . ? You could do a damned sight worse."

Reg Bachelor put a steady gaze on his partner. "Did you hear her screaming at old Dorotea, an' how about her getting into such an argument with the old man he upped and died? Partner, even freckle-faced Elaine is better'n some woman like Flor Calderón. A man would have to sleep with one eye open or wake up with his throat cut. Let's bed down an' get hold of Cleeve tomorrow."

Getting hold of Cleeve wasn't that easy. There had never been scheduled meetings. Cleeve showed up, when it suited him, and he didn't arrive in the village until an afternoon three days later. His reason was believable. The horses were held up by U.S. officials until a veterinarian looked at them. Following that was the fact that Mexico was a land of indifference. It was common knowledge on both sides of the border, but Cleeve said he'd never had to bribe Mexican border people before.

What he said next was met with solemn stares. He would have to deduct the *mordida,* the bribe, from what he'd agreed to pay for the horses to leave Mexico.

Reg growled. "Mister, our job was to catch 'em and deliver 'em to you. After that, they were your horses. You don't deduct bribe money from what you owe us."

Cleeve was momentarily silent before saying: "We don't have a written contract."

This time Reg moved closer. "We shook hands. All three of us understood. We trap 'em, deliver 'em to you, an' you pay the agreed price."

Lane entered the discussion. If Reg got a piece of Cleeve's hide, it wouldn't help. Lane said: "We had help this time."

Cleeve turned on him. "If you agreed to pay for helpers, that's your. . . ."

"It's no different than what you're trying to pull, Cleeve. We'll forget the cost of helpers. You pay for gettin' the horses up to San Diego."

Cleeve had a question. "How much did you have to pay?"

In anticipation of that question Lane said: "The same as you had to pay."

Reg laughed. Cleeve and Lane faced each other until Cleeve said: "Let's go to the saloon. I'll stand the first round."

The partners had to decline. They didn't want to be very far from the trap for any length of time.

As they were parting, Cleeve said: "You two ought to go into the hock-shop business." He smiled. "The truck'll be here in the morning. How many head?"

Reg answered. "Two truck loads. Twenty-two head."

Cleeve's eyes widened briefly before he walked away. "I'll have your money in the morning."

After Cleeve's departure, Reg sourly said: "He'll go to the *cantina.*"

Lane shrugged.

They went over to the trap. Their mustangs were no longer thirsty; they were hungry. The least wary ones went nosing along the ground. They found nothing, and that bothered Lane. Reg read his mind, made a crooked grin, and said: "Where are those Mormons, when we need 'em?"

Like most old, stone troughs this one leaked, and that caused mud daubers to hover. If they stung the horses, it was impossible to tell. Wild horses, particularly hungry ones, move restlessly.

A light breeze stirred the ground cloth, and that started another hoorah among the horses. As hot dust arose, Lane began scratching. Reg said — "Get inside, sluice off." — and grinned. It wasn't meant to be a helpful suggestion. No one in his right mind would try to wash off in an enclosed place full of wild horses.

Horses and men sweated. The sun was a

malevolent, pale color. Distant landmarks shimmered, and a solitary rider, coming from the southeast, appeared to be riding six or eight inches off the ground.

Lane was mopping sweat, when his partner said — "It's old Rosas." — and fished for the makings. "What'n hell does he want now?"

The *mayordomo* was as solemn as an owl, when he reined up, looking at the trapped horses. Without dismounting or looking down, he said: "They go loose."

The partners stared. Reg forgot to light his smoke. Rosas finally looked down. Shaded by his *sombrero* he looked darker. "The *señorita* say you turn the *mesteños* loose and go away from here by tomorrow."

Rosas was uncomfortable. He switched his attention back to the horses, silent and still.

Reg spat out his unlighted cigarette. "Trucks are comin' tomorrow. After that, you tell your *señorita* we'll leave as fast as we can."

The *mayordomo* showed his amiable smile, this time shaded by his hat. "The horses go loose. Go back to wildness."

Reg's gaze at the older man was savage. Before he could speak, Lane said: "She helped us catch 'em."

"*Sí.* Yes, I know." The *mayordomo* shrugged, still wearing his weak smile. "I don't know. She said to me this morning to come over here and turn the horses loose. If you were here, to tell you to free them. To go away from here by tomorrow."

Reg regarded the *mayordomo* for a long moment in silence before turning away. Lane and Hermangildo Rosas watched as Reg saddled his gray horse, swung aboard, and eased over into an easy lope.

The *mayordomo* shook his head, ignored Lane to turn, and left Lane standing there as he rode in the same direction but at a slow walk.

There would be a little daylight left. Lane listened to the hungry horses restlessly moving. He went to the gate, looking in. Several of the mustangs, accustomed to seeing two-legged things beyond the gate, stared without moving. The powerfully built stud horse was one of those staring at the man. Lane talked to him. He tossed his head once or twice, pawed dust to life, and stood his ground.

There was enough light for Lane to notice something neither he nor his partner had noticed before. The heavily maned stud horse had matching small patches of light hair on each side of his withers, the marks of a saddle horse that hadn't had a saddle blanket properly hoisted before the saddle was cinched.

He said: "I'll be damned."

The stud horse didn't move.

Lane looked around. His bay horse was dozing in puny shade. His rigging was up-ended nearby. It was crazy. Even if Reg had been there, what he was thinking was crazy. *Those patches of old saddle sores signified a horse that had been ridden.*

He ducked under the ground cloth, straightened up inside the trap, and the stud horse still didn't move. Lane spoke to it, held out a hand — not a wise thing to do. People feared stallions for kicking. The real danger was biting. That's how stud horses fought, with their teeth. They had several hundred pounds of strength in their jaws. They could take a man's finger off in one pass.

Lane watched the other animals. They shied as far as they could. The stud horse stood his ground. Lane talked to him, ignored time, moved slowly from side to side. Only a fool approached an unaltered horse head on.

It was a meeting of challengers. Lane left the corral, got his saddle blanket and bridle, got back inside with them, waved the blanket, and, when the stallion neither spooked nor moved, Lane went closer on the left side. A wild horse would have swung his rump. This one cocked his head without otherwise moving.

Lane shook the blanket. Nothing happened. He talked his way up close. Horsemen called it "chumming." Lane talked and waited. When the horse turned his head a little, Lane got closer, slowly raised the blanket, and spoke quietly as he eased the blanket in place.

The horse didn't move, but he watched. Lane scratched under his mane, ran his hand over the left side and back, moved clear for the bridle, moved to the left side, raised the headstall with his right hand, and pressed the cheek where the grinders were. The horse opened his mouth. Lane eased in the bit, being careful not to strike teeth, cinched up the throat latch, and let the reins slip through his fingers. The horse could have been a statue.

Lane crawled under the ground cloth, balanced the saddle on one hip, and ducked back inside. The stud horse rolled the bit's copper cricket. He knew what a bit was. Hoisting the saddle into place, easing it down gently, and leaning to catch the far-side cinch were dangerous work. He didn't pull the latigo tight, but stepped back, told the horse they would go outside, and knew the chance he was taking. The moment he dropped the gate, the other mustangs, accustomed to following their leader, would come forward.

He led the stud horse out, turned to pull up the wire, and rearranged the ground cloth. Several of the trapped animals moved warily to follow, but Lane had the ground cloth in place before they got close.

He and the wavy maned Morgan-looking horse gazed at each other. If there were fireworks, if Lane got dumped off, the stallion would run for all he was worth, and maybe his family would charge the gate. The Morgan-looking horse was powerfully muscled up with a short back. When a short-backed horse bucked, it was like straddling an earthquake.

He told the horse, if he bucked hard and got loose with Lane's outfit, when Reg got back, he would explode, and for a fact it was a crazy, pointless thing he was doing.

He turned the stallion twice, rocked the saddle with his left hand, felt the horse hump slightly, rocked the saddle several more times before tightening the right rein until the horse had to turn its head, then he toed in, and came down over leather.

The horse didn't move. His ears were back. That hump under the saddle didn't diminish. When Lane gently tightened his knees against the horse's ribs, the stallion did what had made him free. He tossed his head, got the bit behind his tusks and in front of his grinders, and ran. At any time a runaway saddle animal is dangerous, but with failing daylight the peril was multiplied.

Lane had ridden runaways before, several times. As a youngster he'd been so frightened he'd unloaded. This time he let the horse have its head, made no attempt to control it, and hoped to high heaven the son-of-a-bitch wouldn't stumble over a boulder or fall for some other reason, and used his left rein to ease a change in their direction. If he got lost this far from the trap or, if he met Reg, it would be the end of a partnership.

The stallion wasn't built for speed. He was put together for endurance. Most runaways begin to suck air after a couple of miles. Not this time. They were heading in the direction of the Trinity yard. Somewhere along here Lane expected to see his partner. Whether Reg would be able to stop the runaway was anyone's guess. His gray horse wasn't fast, and the stallion's gait had water coming out of the outer edge of Lane's eyes.

When they came to a drop-off arroyo, the stallion didn't hesitate. After they were on the far side, it occurred to Lane that the horse knew the country. As they topped out on the far side of the arroyo, a scrawny, bitch coyote that was dining on a decaying prairie dog carcass looked up and ran. They swept past as she dove into a thornpin thicket.

Lane could feel the horse slackening. He had no idea how far they had gone, but he guessed it to be maybe five or six miles. He tried the reins, gently. Nothing happened. He let the slack hang until the horse was definitely beginning to scuff with its rear feet, then he tried again, and this time the horse slackened of its own accord. The fight was nearing its end.

Shaggy, old trees were barely visible, dead ahead. Lane drew back a little more until his hard-breathing mount yielded down to a trot. Up ahead a horse trumpeted. The stallion swerved in that direction. There was a weak, yellowish light where a dog barked.

Lane eased the reins again, getting his mount heading for the big, old barn and its hitch rack. His last effort at steering the exhausted stud horse was up to the tie rack.

The horse stood head hung, ribs pumping, sweat dripping.

Lane swung off as a *vaquero* appeared through the barn. Lane held out the reins. "Walk him. Cool him out." A wind-broken horse was useless. The *vaquero* took the reins without speaking and led the stud horse, which followed like a lamb.

Backgrounded by a better light at the main house two people were standing at the verandah's railing like statues. Lane called in that direction. "Reg . . . ?"

The answer came slowly. "What in hell . . . ?"

Lane told a lie he was comfortable with. "Ma'am, you sure know horses. There he is. You wanted him, so I rode him over."

Flor Calderón said something indistinguishable to Reg to which he did not reply as she turned to enter the house. Reg left the porch. The partners met midway between the house and the barn. There were now several other lights from the *chozas*.

Reg looked out where the *vaquero* was walking the stud horse. "He's broke to ride?"

"In a way. He's a runaway. I'd guess that's why someone got rid of him."

"How'd you know I was here?"

"I didn't, except that, when you left the

trap, you headed in this direction." Lane turned to watch the *vaquero* cooling out the wringing-wet stallion. "He brought me. I didn't bring him."

Lane faced his partner as Reg said: "You damned idiot. Who's watching the trap?"

"No one."

"Lane . . . they better be in there when Cleeve and his trucks get there in the morning. Of all the damned fool stunts you ever pulled. . . ."

Flor Calderón called from the porch. Before the partners responded, Lane said: "You two hitch horses?"

Reg was upset and angry. He led the way to the house without speaking until they were almost there, then he stopped, glared. "You gawd-damned idiot!"

Lane smiled. "You're dead right."

"Why'd you do it?"

"He has old saddle gall scars. . . ."

"So you had to try him!"

CHAPTER SEVENTEEN
ADIÓS MÉJICO

Inside the atmosphere was roiled and strained. Lane dropped his hat on a chair, watched the handsome woman go to the old cabinet where her grandfather had stored wine, and draw off three glasses.

She smiled, when she handed Lane his glass. *"Un* buckaroo *bueno,"* she softly said, and smiled.

Reg didn't smile, even if he'd understood. What she'd said could have been a joke, or something else. Her smile meant it had been a joke. When Reg accepted his wine, he and the handsome woman exchanged a long, expressionless look.

When she motioned for Lane to be seated, she put her glass aside untouched and said: "The truck will come tomorrow. Good. After that, the trap will be torn down."

Reg nodded. Evidently this had been agreed upon before Lane arrived. It suited him down to the ground. What else suited him was not mentioned: *Get the hell out of Mexico!*

There was one large glass window in the north wall. It allowed a view of the yard, the buildings, and as far as the curve of this Mexican world. Reg stood looking out the window. He was never very talkative, but now he was even less so. Lane had to guess Reg and the handsome woman had come to some kind of agreement. He was sure of it, when Reg turned and Flor Calderón raised a glass in his direction before sipping.

Reg had always been an easy man to read, to anticipate. Over the ensuing years Lane would come to believe that went with basically honest people. This particular night the handsome woman's manner more than the manner of his partner inclined Lane to believe that whatever they had agreed upon was satisfactory to Flor Calderón but was not entirely agreeable to Reg.

The *mayordomo* rapped softly on the door. Flor nodded for Reg to answer. The older man smiled. "The horse is hungry," he told Reg. "He is cooled out. Do you want him fed?"

Lane answered from where he sat. "No grain, a little water at intervals, and hay if you got it, but no grain."

Flor Calderón went to the door. The *mayordomo* pulled off his hat. She asked if the Lopez *choza* was still empty, and her head rider nodded, without smiling, and whispered something in Spanish which neither *gringo* understood and only just barely heard. She smiled, replied in Spanish, and closed the door. At Lane's expression of inquiry she resumed her seat and reached for her glass. "An old man named Ramón Lopez lived there. He had no family. He is buried in the cemetery not far from where my grandfather is buried. They were close. They grew up together." She sipped and put the glass aside again. "Ramón Lopez died in his sleep in that little house where he'd lived most of his life. They are like Indians. No one will move in where someone has died. Does that bother you?"

Lane shook his head. Since entering the house and sipping the wine he was becoming very tired. His wild horseback ride was partly responsible, but he never would have admitted it.

She arose, a signal the visit was over. She went to the door with them, felt for and held Reg's left hand, and might have risked more if they had been alone. As they crossed the yard, she leaned in the doorway, watching. She only turned back inside when they were no longer in sight.

Hermangildo Rosas was hovering at the barn. He took them to the Lopez house, declined an offer to come inside, and left. There were cobwebs, a musty aroma, and one ancient candle on a tipsy, homemade, small table where Lane placed the lighted candle. There was one bed. It had rope springs and had been built against the south wall.

Reg gestured. "Sleep well," he said and went to the door before speaking again. "Someone's got to be at the trap. For all we know, they've busted out."

After Reg left, Lane shrugged, went to the bed, kicked out of his boots, dropped his hat on the floor, and sank down. Rope springs were bearable, better than either a snowbank or an ant hill.

Horses fighting across a high corral awakened Lane. The sun was up and rising. Within an hour or so the heat would arrive. He washed at a trough and encountered one of the Trinity *vaqueros*. They exchanged smiles. The rider said something Lane couldn't understand and jutted his jaw, Indian fashion.

Lane went to the corral where the runaway stud horse was trading nips with a very large palomino mare. She was horsing or there wouldn't have been a fight. The *mayordomo* joined him, shaking his head.

Except that *el patrón* had been fond of the palomino, it wouldn't have been there. The dark, older man had an equestrian's dislike of mares. Rosas was looking at the stud horse when he said — "The *señorita* has breakfast for you." — and walked away.

On his way to the main house Lane explored how to explain that Reg was gone. She admitted him. Except that the door was wide, he would have been unable to see the wisp of movement where the Pala woman was briskly leaving the kitchen. Inside, the aroma reminded him of food. Flor Calderón looked past as she closed the door.

Lane said: "He went over to make sure the horses don't bust out of the trap."

She nodded, and Lane got the impression that she knew that. She took him to the kitchen, an unchanged relic of earlier generations. There was no stove in the *gringo* sense. It was a stone-built cooking area built into a corner. There was running water, the only modern convenience.

As they moved toward the table and the handsome woman brought a huge platter of food, she asked: "He will come back?"

Lane could answer that easily. "The feller who gets the horses will show up. At least one of us's got to be there to help load."

Flor Calderón had a cup of black coffee. She had already breakfasted. As Lane lit into the meal, she asked a question. "That red-headed woman . . . was she pretty?"

Lane swallowed, looked up, and shrugged. "Not to me, she wasn't. She couldn't hold a candle to you."

The woman softly smiled. "Tell me about him."

Lane concentrated on breakfast. "He was born in Canada. He has two brothers. His father's in the cement business. When we're waiting for spring, we work for him."

"His mother?"

Lane gave up and pushed back his chair. "She's sort of hard to get to know."

"How?"

"She's . . . well . . . not real affectionate."

"And him? He is affectionate?"

That was easier to answer but not truthfully. "Reg likes animals. That gray horse . . . we brought him with us from up north. He . . . I guess you could say he's not exactly a woman's man."

Flor Calderón went after refills for their coffee cups. As she returned, she asked about ranching, and this time Lane had no difficulty.

"He's as good as they come . . . knows cattle and horses." Lane waited until the handsome woman was seated to add: "Up north some folks wanted him to hire on year around as a foreman."

"He didn't?"

"Too cold up there."

"You aren't hungry?"

"Ma'am, it's hard to eat an' talk at the same time."

She laughed, arose to leave the room, and trailed her fingers across Lane's shoulder as she passed. He resumed eating, but most of the hunger had been satisfied. He looked around the big, poorly lighted room and wagged his head. No matter what his partner may have said yesterday, the handsome woman was in for disappointment. If their places had been reversed . . . ? He arose, put on his hat, and walked into the parlor. It was empty, but the old man, *el patrón,* looked stonily at him from the gloom of a wall portrait. Beside him a thin-lipped woman seemed to be looking over his head.

Outside the *mayordomo* and the handsome woman were standing together, watching a lean, hawk-faced, dark *vaquero* ride the Morgan-looking stud horse who obeyed everything his rider reined him to do. Lane smiled. Open the gate and things would be different. The *mayordomo* saw him coming and said something in Spanish. Flor

Calderón also turned.

Lane said: "He's a runaway. Otherwise I couldn't find anything wrong." The *mayordomo* excused himself and went in the direction of the barn. Lane leaned to watch the rider and the stud horse. "Maybe if he was altered . . . ," he said, and Flor Calderón nodded her head.

"He is nine years old by his mouth," she said. "Altering wouldn't change him."

That was true.

She also said: "After the horses are loaded, you could come back with Reg."

That was possible. The idea suited Lane, but he had something in mind. "If I could borrow a horse, I'd like to get back over there."

She called to the *mayordomo* who appeared at the rear barn opening. She told him in Spanish to saddle a horse for Lane, faced the *gringo,* and spoke frankly. "I went to a woman's school in Massachusetts. It took a long time to make the adjustment."

He could believe that. He'd known Yankees. Cleeve, for instance.

"What I learned was useful, but I couldn't unlearn. This is my place, not back there. It's awfully cold in the winters."

The *mayordomo* led a horse bearing Lane's outfit to the rear barn opening.

There was no door and never had been.

She walked with him until the *mayordomo* handed over the reins and turned back into the eternal gloom of the barn. She lay a hand lightly on Lane's arm. "Tell him I'll have supper ready . . . for both of you. Tell him . . . ," — she paused — "tonight can be like last night."

She removed the hand, Lane swung up over leather, smiled, and eased the horse into a steady walk. Some distance out he wanted to look back but didn't do it. He would never see this place again. It required no mystic sensibility to understand that.

By the time he had the trap in sight, it was hot. By the time he dismounted where four men, including his partner, were talking behind two trucks with the slatted sides of vehicles used for hauling livestock, they had seen him. Reg left Cleeve and the truckers. They exchanged a long look before Lane repeated what the handsome woman had said and read his partner's expression correctly. This would be the last time either of them would be in the country. For Lane, at least, this part of it.

The horses were as tucked up as gutted snow birds, but going up the high-sided ramp into the trucks was not something they did willingly. One old mare got down.

The others couldn't jump over her, so they tried to avoid her struggles. Shod hoofs would have made mincemeat out of her. Unshod hoofs did less damage, but, when she was finally able to stand, shaking like a leaf, she was alone in the trap.

Lane yelled for the trucker to slam the door. He told the others to get clear, and, as the old mare came back to solid ground, Lane flung the ground cloth aside, dropped the wire, and waved his hat. The old mare made no attempt to run out of the opening. She walked out. Her injuries would heal in time. She would find another band.

Cleeve came up to say: "That's one shy of twenty-two."

Lane walked away without a word.

Before the trucks got to the border, there would be other injured animals, but in a one-way trip it didn't matter a whole lot. The horses were sweat-dark and wild-eyed. The Mexican truckers were anxious to be on their way. Their wheels stirred up more dust, and Lane's itching started. He went to the trough, shed his shirt, and splashed water with Cleeve and Reg ignoring him as Cleeve counted out the greenbacks for twenty-one horses. He, too, seemed anxious to leave. It was a long drive to the reduction works. Lane was putting on his shirt, when Cleeve called to him. "Let me know when you got another bunch," he said, and climbed into his car and raised more dust as he followed in the wake of the trucks.

Reg came over, counted out half the money, and handed it to Lane. "I got one of those truckers to come back an' haul the gray horse over the border for me." Reg batted at an angry mud dauber. "To get him hauled north from the border'll just about leave me broke." He waited until Lane had pocketed the cash before also saying, "I wish to hell. . . ."

Lane interrupted him. "No you don't, but she thinks you will. In your boots I'd go back, temper or not."

"Then you go back, Lane."

That remark didn't deserve an answer, but Lane gave one anyway. "I don't know what you told her last night, an' it's none of my damned business, but it must have been convincing. She was like a school girl this morning."

Reg used his hat this time, when a wasp came close. He missed, but evidently the winged critter got the idea and flew away as swiftly as it could.

Lane said: "It wouldn't work, anyway. Not you 'n' her. Let's get our traps an' get the hell out of here."

As they went for their horses, Reg asked a question. "What about the horse she loaned you?"

"Turn it loose. It'll find its way home. Reg . . . ?"

"What?"

"Old Dorotea. Give her some money."

"All right."

When they reached the village, there wasn't a soul in sight. Lane smiled. *Siesta* wasn't a bad idea. At least in Mexico.

The stocky blacksmith, Albo Muchacho, with his perpetual smile came out of shade inside his work place and called a greeting in almost accentless English. The partners exchanged a look. The Mexican had got someone to coach him in English.

They left the horses to be washed and fed, promised to return shortly, and walked to the old woman's house. She was out back, sparingly casting handfuls of grain to some runty chickens so infested with lice they'd scratched off most of their feathers. She gestured proudly. She had only the day before bought the chickens, and now she would be able to sell eggs.

They dutifully admired the chickens before she took them inside. The little mud *choza* still smelled of spilt wine. She offered to feed them. They lied with a clear conscience, when they told her they had just eaten. She then offered wine and filled two cups half full and a third cup to the brim. She took that cup to the table with her.

She was in good spirits. Lane noticed that she had also combed her hair. As they sat down, Dorotea fixed Reg with a sharp look. She had seen the trucks pass through but rather than say what she thought she said: "Now you will catch more, no?"

Lane dug out some crumpled *norteamericano* greenbacks, counted out several, and put them in front of the old woman. Her eyes widened. "For what? I am very old and not good to look at."

Reg did the same, matching dollar for dollar. As he pocketed what was left, Dorotea cocked her head slightly, sipped from her cup without moving her gaze from Reg, and put the cup down. "But you will come back?"

Reg had a slight coughing fit.

Lane smiled at the old woman without speaking.

Her eyes narrowed. "Well, it is God's will." She rose and went to a hinged box which she opened and returned to the table to place a barely distinguishable old photograph in front of Lane. He had seen one like it before. The *patrón* had showed it to him. If there was a likeness, he could not recognize it, but then it was not a very good photograph and probably never had been.

Reg picked up the picture, squinted, and put it down.

Old Dorotea half emptied her cup, smiled straight at Reg, and said: "You see it? The likeness to him . . . your friend?"

Under the table Lane nudged Reg's boot. Reg slowly nodded and rose. "We want to thank you, Dorotea."

She started to rise, sank back, and finally managed only when Lane took one arm and hoisted.

It was a boiling hot afternoon before they saddled up and left. It would be much longer before either of them associated the village's name with injured souls, but someone had, generations earlier. St. Teresa, Our Lady of Sorrows had been aptly named.

There was a town called Progresso where two roads passed through, one from the north and one from the east. It was a busy, bustling place totally different from St. Teresa. Because one of Cleeve's truckers had failed to return, they looked for an alternative. They had no difficulty finding a man who owned a small, cattle truck who would haul their horses to the border for six *yanqui* dollars. They could ride in back with their horses. They hired him on the spot, got directions to an eatery, and, after finding the place, were gratified to learn that the proprietor, before being caught and returned to Mexico, had cooked in a Texas restaurant, and he gave them their first genuine *gringo* meal in months.

Lane had an odd thought. "Did you know that deep sea divers are brought back up a little at a time?"

Reg looked around apprehensively. Since they had been partners, Lane had said odd things with seemingly no reason. Reg said: "You read too much."

Lane laughed. "That's us, Reg. From Saint Teresa to civilization by short halts. From day before yesterday to today in halts and starts."

They met the man with the small truck. He had improvised a divider so neither of the horses he was to haul could injure the other. Loading Lane's horse was no problem, but getting Reg's gray in was a battle ending in a tug of war, one Mexican trucker and two *gringo* mustangers at one end of a big rope, the gray horse at the other end, sitting back on his haunches. They finally got him in, made him fast with some slack, and were ready.

The day was dying when they left another dusty road, turned right, and met other vehicles, some with their lights on, although it was not fully night and their driver would not switch on his lights for another hour. His truck had a temperamental battery. Riding in back with two horses, one of which had clearly never been in a truck before and resented being in one now, was not the ideal way to travel, but they were heading in the right direction — and for more trouble. Bringing livestock into the United States from Mexico was not something to be done lightly, particularly since neither Lane nor Reg had bills of sale for their animals.

CHAPTER EIGHTEEN
EL TIEMPO PASA

By the time they reached the border with its opposing sets of buildings — on the Mexican side for those leaving, on the U.S. side for those entering — the area was lighted like a Christmas tree. On the Mexican side uniforms predominated and holstered sidearms.

The trucker pulled off so as not to interrupt the flow of cars. He took the partners to the office of the Mexican *comandante,* who was a stocky, pock-marked, dark man whose neck made it impossible to button his coat to the gullet. He neither introduced himself nor asked the name of the *gringos.* He and the trucker spoke in Spanish, a fluid flow of words with brief interludes of silence.

The officer's underlings came and went. There was only one office, four walls without partitions. The *comandante* needed reassurance the *gringos* were not horse thieves. He and the trucker spoke at length on this subject until the rather slovenly officer shrugged and reverted to English. The fee for taking horses out of *Méjico* was one U.S. dollar a head. Reg dug out two ragged greenbacks and handed them over. The *comandante* handed one *yanqui* dollar to the trucker who grinned like a tame ape as he pocketed the money, winked at the *gringos*, and went outside where he lit a cigarette and waited.

The *comandante* took Lane and Reg outside and around a corner. There, he jutted his jaw in the direction of the U.S. lighted area and said in English, "They will impound the horses. It is their custom. They are afraid horses out of Mexico carry terrible diseases."

Reg scowled. "Impound them? For how long?"

The *comandante* was looking in the direction of the opposite border guard unit when he replied. "Maybe two weeks, maybe two months." He turned, smiling. "It takes them that long to send blood samples somewhere and get back the report. If it is bad, you can't take the horses over the border."

Lane gazed over where the lights were brightest. "Maybe if I walked over there . . . ," he said, and got no further.

The *comandante* was shaking his head. "You can't go over there until I clear you on this side. *¿Comprende, amigo?*"

Reg was not smiling. "You'd keep us here?"

"No. Only long enough. Do you have bills of sale for those horses?"

Lane shook his head, and the officer made a long face. "But it is the law. Over there and over here. How do I know they aren't stolen horses?"

Lane considered the short, bull-built Mexican. He had heard stories about Mexican jails. Prisoners stayed until their teeth fell out. He judged the distance. They could probably cross to the U.S. side if they ducked and dodged as they ran — but that would mean leaving the horses. One look at his partner's face told him Reg would not abandon his gray horse.

There was an alternative. If he guessed wrong on that idea, he could lose his teeth without going to prison, but he had to try it. He smiled and addressed the *comandante* in a combination of both languages. "*¿Señor, cuánto dinero?* How much to go across with the horses?"

The officer broadly smiled. "Twenty U.S. dollars an' five more for the man who will show you the way to get around the *gringo* border."

The *comandante*'s stubby hand was extended. Lane dug out his money, did not have enough so Reg made up the difference, which Reg did showing an expression of suppressed anger. The *comandante* called to the trucker who had been waiting in the dark. He approached, also smiling. The officer handed him five American dollars, and he jerked his head for the *gringos* to follow him. As they turned to obey, the *comandante* called to them wishing them boundless good fortune as he pocketed the *mordida* and returned to the partitionless office.

The trucker said for Reg and Lane to ride up front with him, backed his truck a considerable distance, doused the lights to favor the battery, and drove northward among and around a clutch of houses, most of which showed no lights, broke clear of the last light, and traveled over rough country with the unerring instinct of someone who had done this before. The trucker, like all border people, spoke English as well as Spanish. Better Spanish by far, but understandable English, if one sorted out misplaced words. Lane would one day understand that precise, exact interpretations were impossible, no matter what the language was.

There was a stingy, crooked moon, but poor visibility appeared not to bother the trucker. He drove without lights and also without haste for what seemed half the night but which was actually slightly more than two hours before he halted, grinned, and climbed out.

Unloading Lane's bay was easy. The horse'd had enough rough and rugged truck riding. The gray horse shared that notion, but he came down the ramp like a gray streak. Except that all three men expected something like this, he would have gotten free. As it was, he dragged them with the trucker screaming curses in two languages. When the gray abruptly halted, the trucker considered his rope-burned hands and told the gray horse, if he belonged to him, he would guarantee that his death would be so slow it would require days.

Reg grabbed the Mexican and shook him. "Settle down," he growled. "Which way do we go?"

The trucker raised a thick arm, pointing north. "That way. Be careful. They are out there somewhere. On horses and with lights on their cars. They have boxes that pick up sounds. Good luck."

It only required moments to saddle up. The trucker made a drunken, wide turn and went back the way he had come. Lane looked up. There were a million pinpricks of light up there, and that lopsided moon. There was something else, a silence so deep it was deafening.

They didn't go west. They went north. There had to be a limit to the U.S. Border Patrol's patrolling perimeter. There was, but by morning they saw tire tracks in the area, so they had to go farther. By evening they hadn't seen telltale tracks for several hours, so they turned west and rode all night.

The only thing they encountered was a small band of Mexicans huddled in an arroyo, waiting for a guide to show them how and where they could enter the United States. They saw two distant riders and were wary of them as the riders were of them. Probably they were also *alambristas*.

When false dawn arrived, they continued northward until sunup, then they veered slightly westward. There were occasional buildings, some in small clutches. There was no mistaking their Mexican characteristics, and once they ducked into an arroyo and did not emerge until two boys, minding a mixed band of sheep and goats, would be unable to distinguish anything more than two men on horseback.

It got hot. There wasn't a cloud in the sky. Where they encountered an ancient stone trough, they washed and watered the horses. It bothered Lane that their animals were getting tucked up. Somewhere in this god-forsaken desert country they would have to find horse feed. As loyal and obedient as horses were, they, like the men who rode them, required something to eat, or they would fail, and where the men were riding even the scrub brush and stunted, scraggly trees had been eaten off. Lane said this was goat country, and Reg nodded. By mid-afternoon they began angling westerly. If there was a fence following the borderline, they did not see it.

Lane was beginning to feel safe and said so. Reg didn't respond. He was riding with his head cocked. When he was sure, he said: "Listen."

It was an biplane, not a large one, and it did not fly very high or fast.

Lane looked for cover of which there was none. Scrub brush and those miserable little trees would not conceal men on horseback.

Reg stood in his stirrups. There was an arroyo up ahead. They made for it and got a surprise. At its bottom there was a thin streak of sluggishly moving water. The horses jerked their heads as the partners swung off. Reg was removing the gray's bridle with both reins looped around its neck while it drank, and Lane was preparing to do the same when that little biplane passed to the west. They watched. For some distance it did not alter its course, but eventually it did. As the horses raised their heads with water dripping, the light aircraft made a wide turn and started back. Reg said: "Son-of-a-bitch!" The biplane was flying with a low twist on the left side. It made no effort to disguise its purpose — the two men with horses in a ravine.

There were markings on the side of the biplane, indistinguishable to the watchers in the arroyo. They didn't have to be readable nor did it require any great prescience for the *gringos* to understand why the biplane had made that wide turn before coming back. Reg said: "Well, hell, we can't outrun the damned thing, an' there's no place to hide." He considered his horse. "We're sittin' ducks."

Lane thought they might as well make a run for the border, wherever the damned thing was, and Reg vetoed that. "They'll be waiting." He also said: "If they land that thing, they'll be on foot."

Lane commented dryly. "With rifles."

They snugged up cinches, stepped aboard, and left the arroyo. The biplane seemed to throttle back as it followed them. At its slowest speed it passed overhead. Tired horses did not make good time.

The last sashay the biplane made was low

enough for a man to yell through a bull horn. His words were in Spanish. It required very little sense to know the man was telling them to stop, to halt. Whatever else he said was lost as the biplane moved onward in its southerly course.

Lane said: "Sitting ducks."

Reg pointed. Westerly was a tight scattering of buildings. There were big trees, obviously imported, and what looked to be maybe a mile of wooden fencing. That, too, was unique in an area where useable trees for fencing did not exist.

They decided to head for what they thought might be a small settlement. The closer they got, the more it seemed that it was not a settlement but some kind of ranch. Those big, old trees made shade, and their animals' pace picked up a little. They had caught a scent the men had not: greenery.

The little biplane circled. It made no attempt to conceal the fact that it was interested in the horsemen below. When Lane and Reg were close enough to make a judgment of that ranch, or whatever it was, the little biplane picked up speed and flew in an almost straight line southerly. When they were close enough, they saw green paddocks with sleek, fat horses in them, and the buildings, one of which was a large, long house with a covered ramada completely encircling it, and several smaller structures a fair distance from the main house, close to a large barn, painted light tan possibly to match the surrounding country. The house was interesting, but that barn was a stockman's dream of paradise. It even had a loft door above the large main opening — in a country where no one raised hay.

Reg said: "Whoever in hell he is, he's not hurtin'."

Their approach had been noted by several large dogs and two Mexicans who emerged from the barn and stood like stones as they watched the partners pass the farthest big trees and enter the yard. A large, heavy man came out onto the porch at the big house to lean and also to watch. When the partners were heading for the barn, he turned and called to someone in the house to come out. The second man was also large and massive. Both of them were *gringos*.

Lane swung off and smiled at the Mexicans who were in the barn. He asked if they spoke English. They did, and only one, the graying, older Mexican, had an accent.

Reg explained about their horses, and the older man nodded. He had already made a judgment about the bay and the gray. As he

288

was turning toward the front barn opening, he said: "In here."

The barn had grilled, stall doors and shiny, lower sections. The barn was clean enough to eat off the floor. As the older man said something in Spanish, a younger and taller Mexican went toward an elegantly paneled granary.

The horses were stalled. As the younger man poured ground barley into feed boxes, the older man gave him another order, and after some delay he returned with two thick flakes of pale, green hay which he tossed into mangers. Lane was preparing to say neither he nor his partner had much money when two *gringos* drove up out front, alighted, and entered the barn. Both were unsmiling men of medium height. One of them said: "Obregón sent you?"

Lane and Reg turned. To Lane these two looked more like assassins than ranchers. Both wore suits and neckties. Each had a slight bulge where a shoulder-holstered pistol was concealed.

Lane asked: "Obregón who?"

The matching pair of obvious city dwellers studied the partners without speaking. One of those hefty men from the house entered the barn, jerked his head, and the matching pair returned to their car, made a big sashay, and drove back the way they had come.

The hefty man was smooth-faced, amiable-looking, and smiled as he asked who the partners were. After they told him, he wanted to know where they had come from.

Reg answered. "A place called Saint Teresa, some distance south of here."

The large man with the fixed expression of friendliness said: "What did you do down at Saint Teresa?"

"Trapped mustangs . . . wild horses for a feller named Cleeve who sold them to a reduction works in San Diego."

The big man seemed to be pondering. After a considerable delay he asked another question. "Where are you going?"

Lane answered. "Up to my cabin in the Malibu country."

The large man jerked his head. "Take a walk with me."

He led the way to the main house. Inside it was at least ten degrees cooler than outside. Four men, one a Mexican, arose and left the room as the hefty individual called a name. The man who responded froze Lane and Reg in their tracks. It was Henry Cleeve. He smiled, gestured toward chairs, and told the hefty man to bring some cold *cerveza*.

Cleeve remained standing. "You brought that damned biplane. You boys playing a game with me?"

Reg's temper was rising. "What the hell are you talkin' about? We're on our way to the Malibu country. They told us on the Mex side of the border the U.S. side would impound our horses."

"So you started riding?"

"Yep. A few days . . . far enough to be able to cross back into California."

"Well, you didn't ride far enough. That Border Patrol biplane saw you. They'll come storming into my yard soon. They radioed back to the San Diego headquarters."

Lane finally sat down, tipped back his hat, and looked steadily at Cleeve. "This place belongs to you?" he asked.

Cleeve just looked at him. After a short silence he opened his mouth to speak but was interrupted by a knock on the door. It was one of the stable hands. As Cleeve asked what he wanted, the Mexican stable hand came near. "The horses need a bath," he said.

Cleeve turned and jerked his head for Reg and Lane to go with the stable hand, and the three of them went down to the barn where there was a rack for washing horses with a slatted floor. Reg tapped the older man's arm. The Mexican turned and said softly: "Don't ask questions." In his normal voice he added: "Take that rope and lead your horse to the rack."

The bay and the gray were perfectly willing to be soaked with cool water. The older man soaped and rinsed them both, ignoring the nearby *gringos*. Reg took Lane by the arm as far out back as an overhang above a cement trough full of water. He said: "You want to know what I think?"

Lane shook his head. "Don't look a gift horse in the mouth."

"Cleeve didn't make this place off wild horses."

"You want to take a dip in the trough?"

"No!"

"Reg, leave it be."

Lane turned at the sound of a car. It was actually two cars, both emblazoned with United States Immigration Service emblems on their doors.

The elderly Mexican disappeared. Cleeve and the pair of beefy large men were over on the covered verandah.

Four men piled out of the cars. A short discussion took place, and one man went to the barn. He said his name was Emory Lange. He showed them his identification folder, pocketed it, and started asking questions.

The longer the three of them talked, the more the U.S. federal agent's attitude altered.

Eventually he returned to the house where all four of the U.S. federals conferred, climbed back into their cars, and scuffed dust as they left the yard.

The old Mexican miraculously reappeared. He smiled. *"Bastardos,"* he said. "Always with their noses where they don't belong. I'll tie the horses in the shade to dry."

Late afternoon Cleeve came out back where the partners were sitting in shade. He motioned for them to follow him and led them into the parlor. He was brisk. "All right. When I met you on the reservation, you'd come south from the Saint George country."

Reg interrupted. "We told you all that on the reservation."

Cleeve nodded, told the woman who had entered the room to hand the glasses of beer to his guests, and waited until she had departed before saying: "They overfly me every few days. Today's not one of their days, an' that complicates things. There'll be another plane about two o'clock. He'll come in low, then fly back toward Mexico City."

Lane sipped cold beer, looking straight at Cleeve. He had a question, but prudence told him not to ask it. Instead he said: "That last band of horses arrived in San Diego all right?"

Cleeve's eyes faintly twinkled as he considered Lane. "I wondered if you were as dumb as you look. They arrived. By now they're canned dog food."

Reg said the unthinkable. "Peddlin' wild horses must pay well."

Cleeve's twinkle widened into a smile. "Why the Malibu country?"

Reg replied. "Because Lane's got a cabin up there, an' we need to loaf for a while."

The hefty *gringo* returned to whisper something to Cleeve who nodded without taking his eyes off the partners. After the big man had left, Cleeve went to a chair, sat down, and said: "Why did you come here?"

Reg answered brusquely. "It's the only place we saw that might have feed an' water for our horses . . . Cleeve?"

The wild horse buyer waved Reg off and addressed Lane. "That beaner at the Mex border crossing talked to the man who trucked you fellers. He called down to Progresso. They made a contact in Saint Teresa. Would you like another beer?"

Both partners shook their heads.

Cleeve shoved out his legs and crossed them at the ankles. "Remember when we met on the reservation? You'd been mustangin' up north? Boys, we'll care for your horses. Stay around the yard. If you want, there's a swimming pool out back. I'll see that you're fed." Cleeve shot up to his feet. He was no longer smiling. "All right?"

Reg also stood up. "We'll stay around. We don't have money to pay for the horse feed . . . Cleeve . . . ?"

Cleeve led them to the door and outside. There he said it again. "Don't leave. Loaf for a day or so, until your animals are fit to ride."

The visit terminated when Cleeve went back inside the house. Within five minutes he returned and continued as though there had been no interruption. "You can leave," he said. "If I were you, I'd wait until dark. You're over the line, so all you got to do is head north." Cleeve reached in a pocket, removed a pad of folded money, peeled off two one hundred dollar notes, and handed one to each partner.

Reg looked up. "What's the money for?"

Cleeve's smile returned. "They may contact you. You trapped wild horses for me, that's all. All right?"

Lane nodded. It was Gospel truth.

295

Cleeve shifted his feet, considered the partners briefly, then shook his head, and went back into the big main house.

They were fed at an empty little house by a stone-faced Mexican woman. Afterward, they went outside for a smoke, and Reg leaned as he spoke in a dramatically lowered voice. "You want to know what I think?"

Lane looked around. "No. For the second time, no. It'll be dark directly. Let's look in on the horses."

There were lights at the main house. Among the smaller structures lights were few and muted. Later, as Reg and Lane led their animals out to be saddled, the elderly Mexican did as he'd done before, he appeared soundlessly, almost ghost-like. The partners assumed the older man had been detailed to watch them. He helped with the rigging out, and, as the horses were led outside to be mounted, he offered his last word of advice. "Go west and don't light matches for your smokes. God be with you."

They rode west, and, because the ground was thick with layers of ancient dust and they rode at a steady walk, they made no noise. A mile or two on the way Reg said: "You get a feeling the rocks got eyes?"

Lane laughed. "And ears."

It had to be a pure accident when they

met a trucker with his ramp down. He beckoned, helped load the horses, and did not say a word during one of the longest nights in Lane's life. Not until they emerged from goat tracks that junctured with a paved highway did they both relax, and not for several miles farther along did Reg stop twisting to look out the back window. Once a police car passed. The trucker ignored it, but his passengers didn't. The second police car they saw had Ventura County Sheriff painted on the door, and that meant they were close.

The trucker declined the offer of a smoke and drove like an automaton until the break of day by which time Lane was able to recognize landmarks. They reached the mouth of Yerba Buena Cañon before noon, unloaded, rigged out, thanked the mute trucker, and started up the cañon. They knew they had made it when they passed the mildly elaborate ranch of a motion-picture personality named William Boyd. They had both attended local dances held in an old schoolhouse on the Boyd place — with the owner's permission. One thing that had intrigued Lane was that where Boyd's house sat on a flat place there was a low, stone wall around it. So low even a calvy cow could have jumped over it.

At Lane's topout cabin, not visible from the road, nothing had changed. It was to be expected that ransackers would have found the cabin, but there were still tins of food on the shelves. Cobwebs and mice sign and plenty of dust but otherwise things were pretty much intact.

They hobbled the horses and went inside. The small stove was one of those things that had to be pumped. They worked at it, but the kerosene tank was empty, so they ate a cold supper.

The following day Reg rode to the nearest telephone, made a call, and returned. Mid-morning of the following day his brother — of which he had two — drove in, alighted, considered Reg, and said: "You look like hell." He nodded toward Lane, said he was in a hurry, got Reg into the car, and was ready to leave. Reg called out a window. "I'll be back in a day or two."

Lane cupped his hands. "Bring water."

The nearest spring was a mile distant in a cañon. It was downhill to reach it, but water for all its innocuous appearance was heavy. Carrying two five-gallon cans a mile uphill was guaranteed to make sure that babies were born dead. About nightfall Lane ate, went outside for a smoke, and could see the horses part way down toward a flattened area. It was time to turn the page.

He bedded down inside. He was reconciled to pouring cement for Reg's father. Neither he nor Reg had a trade, unless pouring cement was worthy of that distinction. It paid well. It also encouraged the use of Sloan's Liniment, especially on tender hands and sore backs.

They didn't pour cement. A friend named Roy Horton, who drank like a fish and hadn't been able to get a belt around his gut in ten years, came by. Word got around in the isolated Malibu country. They were hiring actor-riders, called "extras," down at Calabasas. They were also paying for black horses. The picture, according to Roy, was one of those Hollywood spectaculars. When it was finished, it was titled THE CHARGE OF THE LIGHT BRIGADE, and it was a spectacular.

After Reg returned in new clothes, shaved, shorn, and carrying replacement tinned food, the partners went down to Calabasas and were hired on as actor-riders. There was confusion on a grand scale. For one thing, the picture people wanted four hundred black horses. No one had told them, evidently, that really black horses were the rarest of all colored horses. They eventually settled for seal browns. It was said seal browns showed on film as black.

It was hot. In the Calabasas country it was always hot during spring, summer, and fall. Wearing uniforms and big, white gauntlets was bad enough under a boiling sun, but, when the riders were aligned for the charge, Reg looked over his shoulder and softly said: "Jesus Christ! Look back there."

For some reason all those riders behind them who should have been experienced horsemen — weren't. Some were holding their reins in the right hand; some rode squaw bridles, a rein in each hand. There were men sitting on horses with the reins looped so their hands were free.

Reg said: "We're goin' to get killed."

Lane left his place in the rank and turned toward the last row. Reg followed. A short individual with an accent yelled through a megaphone for Reg and Lane to get back in formation, which they did, in the very last row. The charge was a noisy, wild rush, dusty and unpleasant.

The only thing that happened after supper was when one of the extras — her name was Eva Fox — was discovered not to be a man, although in every way that mattered she could pass for one, and someone from the director's staff called out for her to stand up. When she did, he said: "Lady, do you realize there are four hundred men here?"

Eva called back: "Is that all?"

Lane was never happier than when he could shed that uniform and those big gloves.

The balance of the season they worked in a number of movies, mostly Westerns, several with a star of those days named Johnny Mack Brown, who was big enough to throw a saddle on. The pay was good, if the box lunches weren't. Lane bought a yellow and black Studebaker roadster, a wrist watch with diamonds where the numbers should have been, and Reg got pretty well set up, too.

Then the rainy season came. Lane's elegant wrist watch, which he never learned to tell time by, was repossessed, then his car. Outdoor movies, particularly Westerns, were not made when it rained.

El tiempo pasa. Time passes. They poured cement, broke a few horses. Reg married Elaine, the redhead he'd left at the church some time back. Lane got married, bought a house, kept it three years, sold it for more than he'd paid, and bought a piece of income property which he sold for nearly twice what he'd paid for it. He bought acreage, built a fine house, had two sons. Reg was divorced — twice. The partners met to ride in local rodeos. They knocked back a few and remembered other times.

The partnership was ending. Time passes. Reg got another divorce and married number four. Lane did not tell his partner that number four, an Italian woman, was a spitting image of Flor Calderón.

Lane returned to Mexico one last time, not to St. Teresa, Our Lady of Sorrows, but to a place called Mazatlán. Mexico — outlying Mexico, anyway — did not change. It hadn't changed for centuries. Its cities, huge and sprawling and relatively modern, were not Lane's Mexico. He got a surprise and a shock in a village not far from one of those noisy, crowded cities. He met Jacobo, the storekeeper, older and more hunched over. They exchanged an *abrazo,* went to a nearly windowless *cantina,* and ordered a meal.

Jacobo was down there to see a renowned *gringo* surgeon of whom it was said he could work miracles, and Jacobo showed in his face that he needed one. In his back he was never free of pain. It had been there for years, but now it was difficult to live with. Jacobo smiled pensively. It was said *gringo* surgeons knew the secret arts of curing. They were not to be compared with *curanderos.*

They sat outside with a full moon, a bottle of wine, and talked. Jacobo asked about Reg and nodded each time Lane told him of Reg's four marriages. He said: "Old companion, your friend is not a woman's man. He is a man's man. That kind. . . ." Jacobo shrugged and asked a question. "Do you remember Flor Calderón?"

"As long as I live, I will remember her. Why? She is married?"

Jacobo emptied his glass before replying. "She never married." Jacobo cleared his throat. "And Dorotea Saenz. She died long ago. And the *mayordomo,* Hermangildo Rosas. He, too, is dead. Here, we'll split what is left." They emptied the bottle, saluted, and emptied their glasses.

Jacobo wiped his mouth. "Her son is named Aguinaldo for her father. You didn't know him. He was a fine. . . ."

"What are you talking about? Whose son?"

Jacobo answered quietly. "Flor Calderón's son. He is a fine boy. Our village now has a resident priest. Do you plan to visit Saint Teresa?"

Lane was recovering from shock, when he

shook his head. "No."

Jacobo could not sit long in one position, so he shifted as he spoke again. "The horse trap is gone. Do you remember Albo Muchacho? He no longer shoes horses. Too fat. He has more children. He drinks too much and likes to tell stories. Some of them are about his *gringos compañeros* of whom he was very fond and who he helped in all things." Jacobo turned his head. He was smiling again. "About young Aguinaldo, there has been talk in the village that maybe your partner will come back. It would be good, if he did."

They parted with another *abrazo*, and this time Jacobo flinched. He lied in good conscience. "It is the wine. It increases the pain."

Lane returned home, bought and sold property until he could buy a small ranch, and built a wonderful house with corrals and a handsome barn. He sold out that time for more money and went north to buy a larger ranch with water running past it.

Reg Bachelor drove in one day. It was good to see his old partner. They shook hands and slapped each other on the back. Male *gringos* do not embrace, no *abrazo*.

Reg had heard of a ranch for sale in Idaho. They sat in tree shade. Lane mentioned meeting Jacobo. That was all he said of his last visit to Mexico.

The following day Reg went to find his ranch in Idaho. Whether he found it or not, Lane never knew. Outside of the town of Sand Point in Idaho, Reg pulled his car to the side of the road, switched off the ignition, locked his hands around the steering wheel, put his head down, and that was how he was found the next day — dead.

Lane had one more page to turn. A newspaper account of a multi-million-dollar drug cartel that was headquartered down near the U.S.–Mexican border, owned and operated by a man named Henry Cleeve. His assets, including the magnificent ranch, were confiscated. He was heavily fined and imprisoned for three years. When he was released, he went to England to live. He had been born in England.

Lane was sorry his old partner couldn't have stuck around a little longer. Neither of them had believed Cleeve wasn't involved in something illegal. In a lifetime Cleeve couldn't have acquired the kind of money it would take to create that desert paradise, buying wild horses others trapped for him.

ABOUT THE AUTHOR

Lauran Paine who, under his own name and various pseudonyms has written over nine hundred books, was born in Duluth, Minnesota, a descendant of the Revolutionary War patriot and author, Thomas Paine. His family moved to California when he was at an early age and his apprenticeship as a Western writer came about through the years he spent in the livestock trade, rodeos, and even motion pictures where he served as an extra because of his expert horsemanship in several films starring movie cowboy Johnny Mack Brown. In the late 1930s, Paine trapped wild horses in northern Arizona and even, for a time, worked as a professional farrier. Paine came to know the Old West through the eyes of many who had been born in the previous century, and he learned that Western life had been very different from the way it was portrayed on the screen. "I knew men who had killed other men," he later recalled. "But they were the exceptions. Prior to and during the Depression, people were just too busy eking out an existence to indulge in Saturday-night brawls." He served in the U.S. Navy in the Second World War and began writing for Western pulp magazines following his discharge. It is interesting to note that all of his earliest novels (written under his own name and the pseudonym Mark Carrel) were published in the British market and he soon had as strong a following in that country as in the United States. Paine's Western fiction is characterized by strong plots, authenticity, an apparently effortless ability to construct situation and character, and a preference for building his stories upon a solid foundation of historical fact. ADOBE EMPIRE (1956), one of his best novels, is a fictionalized account of the last twenty years in the life of trader William Bent and, in an off-trail way, has a melancholy, bittersweet texture that is not easily forgotten. MOON PRAIRIE (1950), first published in the United States in 1994, is a memorable story set during the mountain man period of the frontier. In later novels he has shown that the special magic and power of his stories and characters have only matured along with his basic themes of changing times, changing attitudes, learning from experience, respecting nature, and the yearning for a simpler, more moderate way of life.

We hope you have enjoyed this Large Print book. Other Thorndike Press or Chivers Press Large Print books are available at your library or directly from the publishers.

For more information about current and upcoming titles, please call or write, without obligation, to:

Thorndike Press
P.O. Box 159
Thorndike, Maine 04986 USA
Tel. (800) 223-1244 or (800) 223-6121

OR

Chivers Press Limited
Windsor Bridge Road
Bath BA2 3AX
England
Tel. (0225) 335336

All our Large Print titles are designed for easy reading, and all our books are made to last.